J

**W9-AGY-797**

# Darling

**Mercy Dog of World War I**

# Darling
## Mercy Dog of World War I

Written by Alison Hart
Illustrated by Michael G. Montgomery

PEACHTREE
ATLANTA

Ω

Published by
PEACHTREE PUBLISHERS
1700 Chattahoochee Avenue
Atlanta, GA 30318-2112
www.peachtree-online.com

Cover design by Nicola Simmonds Carmack
Book design by Melanie McMahon Ives

Cover illustration rendered in oil on canvas board; interior illustrations in pencil. Title,
byline, and chapter headings typeset in Hoefler & Frere-Jones's Whitney fonts
by Tobias Frere-Jones; text typeset in Adobe's Garamond by Robert Slimbach.

Printed in August 2013 in the United States of America by RR Donnelley & Sons
in Harrisonburg, Virginia

10 9 8 7 6 5 4 3 2 1
First Edition

Library of Congress Cataloging-in-Publication Data

Hart, Alison, 1950-
Darling, mercy dog of World War I / by Alison Hart.
        pages cm
Summary: In Cosham, England, in 1917, Darling, a mischievous collie, must leave
the children who love her when she is chosen for training as a mercy dog, seeking out
injured soldiers on the battlefield and leading medics to them.
ISBN-13: 978-1-56145-705-2 / ISBN-10: 1-56145-705-1
  1.  Collie—Juvenile fiction. 2.  Search dogs—Juvenile fiction. [1. Collie—Fiction. 2.
Search dogs—Fiction. 3. Dogs—War use—Fiction. 4. Soldiers—Fiction. 5. World War,
1914-1918—Fiction.]  I. Title.
  PZ10.3.H247Dar 2013
  [Fic]—dc23
                                         2012050991

*To all the brave and dedicated working dogs*
*—A.H.*

*For my dogs—*
*devoted and steadfast companions*
*through the years*
*—M.G.M.*

# CONTENTS

## CHAPTER 1

# Runaway

February 1917

**D**arling is going to be a nurse," Mistress Katherine said. I felt a tug on my collar as she pulled me toward her.

"Darling is going to be a soldier!" Master Robert declared. A harder tug yanked me toward him.

Katherine set a pretend nurse's cap on my shaggy head. "The British soldiers need Darling to care for their wounds," she insisted.

"No, silly goose." Robert whisked away the cap and replaced it with a heavy helmet. "She will be in the trenches on the Front, fighting."

The three of us were in the fenced yard behind "home," a small brick house in the village of Cosham in England. A pigeon flew from the eaves and flapped over my head. I leaped up, trying to catch it, and the helmet toppled to the ground.

Katherine grinned. "See? Darling doesn't want to be a soldier." She reached for the nurse's cap, still in Robert's hand. "Give it to me, please."

"Never." Robert tossed the cap into the rosebush. "She will be a sergeant, like Father."

"Oh, you brute! Mummy!" Katherine hollered as she ran for the back door.

Another pigeon fluttered from the eaves. I jumped, and it soared upward. Ears pricked, I raced after the bird as it glided over the picket fence. I dove beneath the rosebush. The thorns snagged my fur but couldn't get through the thick rough of my coat. Working furiously, I widened the hole I had been digging for days.

"No, Darling." Robert grabbed my collar. "You mustn't run off. Father is leaving for France this morning. We have to say goodbye."

Dirt flew from beneath my paws. Tugging free from Robert's grasp, I crawled under the fence. Rags met me on the other side, his terrier whiskers bristling with excitement. We raced down the dirt lane. Pigeons burst from sidewalks and stoops, taunting us.

No pigeon could escape us! Rags and I darted right and left. Turning the corner, Rags led the way up High Street.

"Get outter the way, you mutts!" Cart wheels barely missed my paw. A burlap sack of last year's potatoes fell onto the walk in front of me. Thomas, the fruit seller's cob, whinnied. His hooves danced and his harness jingled as if he wanted to gallop away with us.

In the distance, I heard Robert and Katherine calling. But I was tired of playing soldier and nurse. Running free was too fun.

A horn honked as we crossed the cobbled road. Tires screeched. A cane whacked at my head. The baker's boy yelped as we wound around his legs. Rags zipped past the post office.

Sparky the postmaster's dog used to bark from the doorway when we went past. Sweet from the dress shop would chime in with her yips. *Where were they now?* Lately, Rags's and my barks were the only ones to be heard.

I lifted my muzzle in the air. The smell of meat and marrow teased my nose.

*The butcher's boiling bones!* We both knew what

that meant. Bones to steal. Bones to gnaw. Bones to bury.

Rags tossed a "hurry up" bark over his shoulders. Panting, we careened down Wayte Street and stopped at the back corner of the shop. A huge cast-iron kettle steamed over a wood fire. There was no sign of the apron-clad butcher and his cleaver.

Rags crouched in the shadows around the corner. I waited politely by the back door. My ears pricked when it creaked open.

"Aye, Darling, you artful beggar. Are you looking for a bit of a treat?" the butcher asked.

I sat back on my haunches and lifted my paws prettily.

Plucking two bones from the pot with bare fingers, he tossed them to me. "Don't be wasting them now. Times are hard since food's been rationed, and the winter's been so cold." He sighed. "I wish this bloody war would end."

Rags darted out, snatched a hot bone, and ran off. I barked a thank-you. Delicately, I picked up my bone between my teeth so as not to get burned and trotted after him. He was hiding behind a barrel, gnawing greedily. Rags had grown wary of the police, who shot strays. Since he had no family, he was always hungry. I dropped my bone by his front paws. I knew he would bury it for later.

Leaving Rags to his treat, I made my way back to High Street. I *did* have a family. I thought of Robert and Katherine, calling after me. My heart tugged in the direction of home. But my nose pointed north to the sheep pasture just beyond the village.

Excitement made me trot briskly. Sheep were in my blood. My mum herded on a farm on the outskirts of Cosham. Before my new family had taken me home to live with them, I herded too.

Past the Railway Hotel, I broke into a run. Portsdown Hill rose in the distance. Sheep dotted the brown foothills like specks of snow. I dashed up the tram line. I heard clattering and clanking and looked over my shoulder to see the emerald green streetcar. It barreled toward me on its way over The Hill. I scooted off the tracks to let it pass. Sheep flowed away from the racket in a wave of white.

"Darling!"

"Oh, do be careful!"

Robert and Katherine stood on the other side of the tracks, waving and shouting. They had put on mittens and caps against the cold.

*Caught!* I trotted over the tracks toward my children. My tail was tucked. My ears drooped as I tried to look sorry for running off. Katherine and Robert hurried toward me.

"Naughty girl!" Robert tied a rope to my collar. "It's a wonder Farmer James hasn't shot you. We must hurry now and get to the train station. Father is shipping off for France."

"Even though he shouldn't go to war." Katherine sounded like Mum. She pulled me close and made sure the knot in the rope was tight. "Father is simply too old. Come along, Darling. Mummy's waiting at the train station with Baby. She's been weeping ever since Father volunteered."

I cast a wistful glance at the sheep. I didn't care about Father shipping off. I didn't care that Mum was weeping. I didn't care about war and hard times. But I followed Katherine and Robert, wagging my tail and pretending that I did.

Until I could run away again.

## CHAPTER 2

# Farewell

February 1917

*Scree-ee-ee-eech!* The squeal of the locomotive hurt my ears. I crouched on the platform by Katherine's side, wishing I was off with the sheep. Mum wore her best coat. Baby's wool bonnet was decorated with British flags.

Behind them stood Father, dressed in khaki. I knew this was his uniform because Robert often tried it on and marched around his attic bedroom when no one but me was looking. Father's back was straight. He frowned when he saw me.

Smoke and steam filled the air. *Squee-ee-ee-al!* Slowly the locomotive braked to a stop, the noise drowning out Katherine's and Mum's sobs.

Soldiers milled around us, waiting to depart. I barely recognized the livery boy in his new army uniform, even though he used to chase Rags and me from the stable every morning. The tailor's son, the green grocer, and the pastry cook at the inn who sometimes threw us scraps were also dressed as soldiers. None of them paid me mind now.

As a group of soldiers boarded the railway car, cheers rang out. Robert and his friends waved flags and some young ladies held up a banner. The men in uniform gave their last goodbyes. Their smiles were brave, but I could sense their fear.

Father hugged Katherine. "Don't cry, my pet. With these fresh recruits, the war will be over by Christmas. I'll be home with presents."

"A doll from Paris?" Katherine asked between snuffles. "With a lace skirt?"

Robert dropped on one knee next to me. "Darling, look." He pointed to four soldiers standing like a row of trees alongside the nearest railcar. "See their rifles? They're guarding us from the Germans."

"Robert." Father's tone was grave.

Robert jumped to his feet. "Yes, sir."

"You must be the man of the house." Father stuck out his hand and the two shook. "Mother will need your help."

"Yes, *sir!*" Robert saluted him. "And soon I will join you at the Front."

Father chuckled. "The war will not wait for you to turn eighteen."

"Geoffrey the chimney sweep enlisted at sixteen," Robert declared.

"Without his parent's permission," Mum said sternly. "And you are but twelve."

"All aboard!" The conductor's shout rang down the platform.

Father held Mum one last time. Baby squalled; he

hated the noise as much as I did. "Christmas, then," Father told her. "They are saying the war will be over before year's end. That's only eight months."

Mum nodded, her eyes red. Then she stepped back, Baby clutched tightly in her arms. Father patted my head as if forgiving me for running off. "Watch over them, Darling," he said before climbing the steps to the railcar.

"Goodbye, Father!" Katherine waved a lace handkerchief. As the locomotive began to move, Robert snatched my rope from his sister's hand. Together, we wove through the cheering onlookers, toward the end of the platform. Several soldiers swung aboard at the last minute. The giant steel wheels groaned as the train picked up speed.

"Next stop, Portsmouth!" the guard shouted from the top of the railcar's steps.

"Do you see him, Darling?" Robert asked. I scanned the open windows for Father's face, barking when I spied him.

"Goodbye, Father!" Robert hollered. "Goodbye!" Stopping at the end of the platform by the stacked freight, he waved at the departing train.

Brown shapes scurried among the wooden crates. My nose twitched. *Rats!*

I took off, tearing the rope from Robert's grasp. Dashing between the boxes, I went after the rats. But those pests were quick and clever. If Rags was here, they would have no chance. He caught and killed them with a snap of his jaws. I dashed toward them, but they outwitted me, disappearing in the dark crevices.

I needed Rags's help and I knew where to find him. Head low, I sneaked away from the clatter of the train on the rails. I made my way to the outskirts of Cosham. By day, Rags often hid in the chalk pits on Portsdown Hill, away from the dogcatcher's net. It was an easy run for me.

When my nose picked up the scent of the sheep, my pace picked up too. Soon I spied them grazing on the slope. I sunk to my belly and crept along the brown grass, eyes keen. One sheep lifted his head. Then another. They began to trot up the hill and I followed them, circling around the herd.

*Go this way!* I told them with a nip at their hocks. *No, go that way!* Confused, they bleated and began to trot faster.

Suddenly I heard the crack of a gun. *Farmer James!*

"Be off, you bloody mongrel!" Another crack.

I slipped into the middle of the herd, winding among the sheep so Farmer James couldn't get a clear shot at me. Rope trailing, I plunged through the cowslip, keeping low. Ahead of me were rows of white tents along the swell of Portsdown Hill. Soldiers sat on camp stools and cleaned rifles. Rags and I used to beg at the camp, and the soldiers—training far from home—had been friendly. But things had changed and their faces had grown sterner. Today these soldiers might be as unfriendly as Farmer James.

I ducked into a thicket of hawthorn and wild privet and peered out from under the branches. There was little cover between here and the chalk pits, but once there I would be safe. Still staying low, I darted toward the hills. Suddenly, I was jerked flat. *The rope!* The loose end was snagged between two hawthorn branches.

I scrambled to my feet. *Voices.* Someone was coming. I tugged furiously, hoping to dislodge the rope, but it wouldn't budge.

"Looks like he's got himself stuck."

*The voices were coming closer.* I yanked harder. The knot was beginning to tear free when strong fingers wrapped around my collar.

"Aye, lad. Quit your pulling." The rope lifted and I was jerked from the brush. Wagging my tail, I looked up, hoping neither of the faces were Farmer James or Constable Cornwall. Two soldiers stared down at me, their caps tipped back.

"He's a handsome one," said the man holding my rope. "Has a collar and looks well fed. He must not be a stray."

"Though someone was shooting at him. I bet he's run off." The other soldier looked me over carefully.

"Hello, this isn't a he...this is a *she*. Isn't this the collie we named Lassie who comes begging with her mate? The one who comes round with two children from the village?"

"What should we do with her? If the farmer or police catch her, they're bound to shoot her."

"Or the dogcatcher will pack her off to Battersea Dogs Home."

"I heard the army takes the dogs that end up there. Turns them into war dogs."

I licked the soldier's hand and whined. He laughed. "She's telling us she doesn't want to go to war. I know exactly how you feel, lass."

"Let's turn her loose then. She'll find her way." The second soldier crouched. "You head home, girl. Dogs all across England are being shot or sent to homes now that the dog tax is so high. Your family must love you a lot to pay it. So go on now."

He untied the rope. I circled twice, barked a thank-you, and ran off. This time I sped straight toward Cosham village. I hadn't understood all the talk about

Battersea Dogs Home and war dogs. But I knew that I was lucky. It might have been Farmer James who had caught me—and he would not have spared my life.

**CHAPTER 3**

# Letters from Father

Beginning of March 1917

**T**his is a jolly good day for you, Robert," Mister Crispin said when we entered the post office. He pushed a small stack of envelopes across the counter. "You have two letters from your father."

Robert's eyes shone eagerly as he took them. "Is one addressed to me?" he asked.

"It is." The postmaster chuckled and leaned over the counter. "Good day to you, Miss Darling," he said to me. "Are you going to join your master in the war?" He pointed to a bulletin tacked on the wall. "The British Army is using dogs as well as lads."

"Really?" Robert led me over to the bulletin. It showed a dog standing proudly on a hill. Bombs blasted behind him. "See Darling? That German shepherd is a soldier. I told Katherine you could be one."

"They don't call them *German* shepherds anymore," Mister Crispin said. "They call them Alsatians. On account of us hating the Huns since the war started."

Robert read aloud from the poster. "'Even a Dog Can Aid the War Effort. Why Not You?'" He puffed out his chest. "I would go in an instant, Mister Crispin," he declared.

"I too. But alas, I am old with poor eyesight and flat feet. Now hurry home. Your mum will be anxious for those letters. You let me know how your father is faring."

"Look, Darling, one *is* addressed to me!" Robert said. I trotted beside him as he hurried to the top of High Street. Sitting on the chemist shop's stoop, he carefully opened the envelope and pulled out a sheet of paper.

"'Dear Robert,'" he read. "'Mother writes that you and Katherine are working hard at your studies and properly doing chores. Thank you for being a good son. She tells me that Darling is still running off and that Farmer James has complained about Darling worrying the sheep.'"

Robert frowned. "I told Mum not to tell Father about that. You don't hurt the sheep. And you always come back...right, girl?"

I laid my head on his leg. My muzzle twitched; I could smell meat from the butcher's. Lately, all Katherine fed me was a boiled egg or bread soaked in milk. The butcher had been tossing fewer bones as well. I licked my lips. My mouth watered for shepherd's pie and minced beef.

Robert ruffled my ears as he continued reading. "'The French Armies use dogs, and the British are training them, too. Messenger dogs are smart and swift. Sentry dogs are keen and brave. Darling would be fine at either. I know this will be hard for you and your sister, but the dog tax has gone up to ten shillings, and we can no longer afford to keep her. I have written Mister Seligman, the area recruitment officer. He will be coming round to the house to pick up'"—Robert gasped—"'to pick up Darling'!" He leaped to his feet, startling me. "What is Father saying? That you are to go to war? I won't allow it! Father says I am in charge. I'll tell Mum we need you here."

Tugging my rope, he raced down the lane toward home. Robert seemed upset, but I was happy to be off with him.

"Mum! Katherine!" Robert hollered as we rounded the corner. Mum stood on the front walk, talking with Missus Ketchum from next door. Katherine leaned over Baby's pram. "Who's my wittle ducky?" she cooed.

I skittered to a halt as Missus Ketchum swung round, glaring at me. "There's the scalawag that done this!" She held up a white pillow slip and lacy undergarments, all streaked with dirt.

"And you can't play innocent. Look 'ere." She held a petticoat under Robert's nose, and he flushed. Brown paw prints dotted the fabric. "It don't take Sherlock 'olmes to figger out 'oo's guilty."

I slunk behind Robert. Rags had been the one to pull down the wash, but I had joyfully trampled it.

"I am so sorry, Missus Ketchum. We try to keep her from running loose." Mum's face was dark with anger. "Robert, take Darling inside and lock her in the cellar."

"Yes ma'am." Head low, Robert led me into the house and down the narrow hall. He opened the door of the dank cellar. I hesitated, not wanting to go down the narrow steps. "You have made Mum furious, Darling. When Mister Seligman comes, she'll be only too eager to be rid of you." He sighed deeply.

"Robert?" Katherine whispered. I turned around quickly. She had followed us down the hall so silently that I hadn't sensed she was there. "What's wrong?"

"Darling is going to war." Robert's choked out.

Katherine's eyes widened. "What do you mean?"

"Father has told the recruitment officer to pick her up. She'll be trained as a messenger dog or sentry. She'll be shipped off to France, just like Father."

Katherine's eyes filled with tears. "I thought that was what you wanted." She kneeled beside me and buried her face in my fur. "You said you wanted her to be a soldier and go to the Front."

"That was pretend." Robert leaned down to pet me. "If Darling leaves, I'm afraid she'll never come back."

"Then we'll help her run away." Katherine began to unknot the rope from my collar. "She'll live in the chalk mine with Rags. He'll know how to hide her from the recruitment officer. We'll bring them bread and bones when we can."

Robert took her hand off the rope. "No. I wouldn't want Darling to end up in the Battersea Dogs Home. I suppose Father is right. This is best. Darling hates being penned in the yard and locked in the cellar. She's smart and fast. The poster at the post office shows a war dog. That could be Darling."

"Is that what you want, girl?" Katherine held my face between her fingers and I licked her chin. "Do you want to serve with Father's regiment and save his life?"

Robert nodded. "Yes, she does. She'll protect Father from the Germans, and both will come home heroes."

"I thought I told you children to lock Darling in the cellar," Mum said as she strode down the hall, Baby tucked under one arm like a package. I wagged my tail but she didn't even glance at me as she went into the kitchen.

"We can't now," Robert said, following her. "Darling needs to get ready to go to war."

"What nonsense are you nattering on about?" Mum plopped Baby in his high chair and handed him his bowl of gruel. He promptly threw his spoon to the floor. I got two or three licks off it before Katherine scooped it up. "Be good now," she warned me in a low voice. "So Mum will forget about locking you in the cellar."

"Two letters came from Father." Robert thrust them at Mum. "One was addressed to me."

Mother's face paled and she slumped onto the nearest chair. "Is…is he all right?" she stammered.

"He's fine," Robert said as she took the letters.

Carefully she tore open the one addressed to her. She read it to herself, her face turning pink again. Then she read the one addressed to Robert. Katherine and Robert stood quietly, watching her. Baby flailed his arms and dumped over his gruel. When no one paid any mind, I licked up the drips running down the legs of the high chair.

Finally Mum's shoulders relaxed and she smiled. "Yes, he is fine. He made the crossing over the Channel and is stationed in France. He mustn't say where he is in case the Germans get ahold of his letter." She held out her arms. "He also sends this hug."

Katherine and Robert fell onto her lap. Barking, I wiggled between them.

"Did you read the part about Darling?" Robert asked.

Mum nodded. "It is sad, but it's for the best. Everyone has to sacrifice in wartime—even dogs and children." Mum patted my head, and I poked my muzzle into her lap, glad that she'd forgiven me. But then Katherine began to cry. I snuffled her cheek, wondering what was wrong.

"I'm sorry, dear, but the war has changed everything. So it is for the best," Mum repeated quietly.

And this time I heard the sadness in her words.

## CHAPTER 4

# The Final Stop?

March 1917

**W**hoo-whoooo! A whistle sounded and I toppled sideways, hitting the wall of my wooden crate as the train slowed. Scree-ee-eech! This time I wasn't on the platform saying goodbye. Instead I was inside a rattling, swaying railcar.

I righted myself, circled, and lay down, trying to get comfortable in the musty straw. Above, beside, and below me, more dogs in crates barked. I heard the deep woofs of large mastiffs, the shrill yaps of small terriers.

The brakes made a loud hiss, and the train drew to a stop. The barking became more frantic, as if the dogs were begging to be set free. The train had stopped many times before, and no one had freed us, so I tried not to get my hopes up.

Voices came from outside, and the whines and barks rose into a chorus. *Is this home?* they asked. *Are we finally home?*

I closed my eyes. I was hungry, tired, and cramped. A low whine escaped from deep in my own throat. Where we were going, I had no idea. But I had sensed from Katherine's fierce hug and Robert's teary farewell that this train was not taking me home.

"Shoeburyness!" The cry woke me from a restless sleep.

I knew what shoes were—they tasted delicious—and of course I understood the word "bury." Was this our final stop? My stomach growled. I was so thirsty that my tongue was dry. No one had fed or watered us in what seemed like forever. I couldn't tell how long we'd been locked inside the noisy railcar.

"All passengers for Shoeburyness!"

The train eased to a stop, and I heard clanking and scraping noises. Suddenly the heavy door slid open. Sunlight poured in, making me blink. A chorus of barks rang out around me. *Let me out! Let me out! I'm hungry. I'm thirsty. I'm tired.*

I stayed silent.

"Settle down, you mongrels." The voice did not sound angry. "Your 'andlers'll be 'ere in a spit to get you out."

I tried to see through the air holes in my crate. A group of men stood in the doorway of the freight car. They were dressed in uniforms like Father. Each held a leather leash in his hand.

"A good lot," one said heartily. "At least two dozen. The War Office message in the newspapers must have stirred folks into donating their dogs."

A second man chuckled. "That and the increase in the dog tax. Only wealthy gents and ladies can afford their lurchers and lap dogs."

"Let's get these unloaded, men!" someone called out.

Paws drummed above me as the dogs realized they

were being released. Others dug wildly at the wooden doors. I crouched against the back of the crate and hid my muzzle in the corner. These men weren't Katherine and Robert. And this place smelled of fish, not of sheep. Oh, how I wished I was home.

I heard dog after dog leap from the railcar. Finally the din receded. "I think there's one dog left." A man peered into my cage.

"Must be hiding, Sergeant," a second man said. "Or sick. Hasn't made a peep."

The latch ratcheted back and the door opened. "Aye, beauty, are you homesick? I'm Sergeant Hanson."

The other man laughed. "You'll be shaking 'ands with 'im next."

"Perhaps I will, Private Kent." Sergeant Hanson held his hand under my nose. "You've got to be hungry."

A small bit of dried beef was in his palm. I hadn't had a meat scrap since long ago. Still wary of him, I took it carefully.

"Dainty one, aren't you?" He smiled. "Must be a

lady among all these gents." His fingers found my collar and hooked a leash to the ring. "Look, there's a note attached. Come on, girl. I know you've got to relieve yourself."

Slowly I crawled from the crate and jumped to the wooden platform. I was stiff, but I strained at the leash when I saw a grassy plot outside. I did my business, ducking behind a gaslight pole for privacy.

The Sergeant led me to a bucket of water. While I drank, he read the note aloud. *Dear soldier. This is Darling. She is smart and brave. Please take care of her and send her home to us. We love her even though she runs away sometimes. Yours truly, Robert and Katherine.*

"Darling?" Private Kent snorted. "That name'll send fear straight as an arrow into those black German hearts." He held the leash of a large white and tan hound with floppy ears. Raising his head, the hound bayed, then leaped and tugged at the leash. Most of the other dogs and handlers were off in the distance, walking down the lane.

"Hello then, Darling." Sergeant Hanson folded up

the letter and slid it into his pocket. "You remind me of my own dog when I was a boy." He stroked my head. "We were sheep farmers outside of Surrey. Come, lass. Let's see how well you know commands." He started walking and said, "Heel!"

I knew the command well. I fell into step beside Sergeant Hanson's side, eyes keen. The four of us set off down the lane. The hound circled Private Kent, tangling the leash in his legs. As we left the station, I checked the railway tracks that wound through a marshy field. That was the pathway to home.

After a good meal I would be off, trotting the rails back to Cosham. The train ride had seemed endless, but my legs could carry me for hours.

We followed the lane past a row of small shops. One smelled like the Cosham bakery and my stomach growled again. As we left the village, the ground under my paws became sandy and the smell of fish grew stronger. Birds swooped overhead. Larger than pigeons, they were white and gray with orange bills. They eyed me as if unafraid.

It was then I saw the water, which stretched as far as I could see. Its vastness reminded me of Portsdown Hill, except it was gray, and there were no sheep. I stopped, my nose high, drawing in the chilly, briny air.

"That's the North Sea you smell," the sergeant said to me. "Up ahead the River Thames flows into it. The training school isn't far."

"Maybe a map would 'elp 'er figger out where she is," Private Kent called over his shoulder as the hound dragged him past us.

"It might be you who'll need the map when your charge pulls you clear to London," Sergeant Hanson replied with a laugh.

We continued on, the ground growing mucky and slick in places. A large building surrounded by walls stood on a hill in the distance. I heard barking and howling coming from the other side. I pricked my ears. Was this another railcar taking me even further? Or a place for naughty dogs who chased sheep?

We rounded the wall. The hound ahead of me

suddenly stopped and growled ferociously, then lunged backward, yanking Private Kent off his feet. "Whoa, you beast!" he ordered as he struggled to regain his footing in the mud.

Sergeant Hanson chuckled. "Beast is a good name for that one. Perhaps he can be trained to pull artillery."

Tongue lolling and frothy, Beast plunged right and left. I stepped back as Private Kent reined him in with the leash. I trembled, wondering what Beast had seen that caused such a wild reaction.

"Nothing to fear. Come." Sergeant Hanson strode forward and past the wall. Before us stretched a field striped with row after row of wooden crates. Tied to each crate was a dog—some small and large, some fuzzy and floppy. There were more dogs than had once lived in the whole village of Cosham, and they were frantically barking as they jumped on and off the crate roofs.

The other handlers and dogs had arrived from the railway, adding to the frenzy. I heard barks of greeting,

but I also heard howls of unhappiness and growls of anger and fear.

Cosham had gradually grown empty of dogs. Was this where they had gone? Tucking my tail, I pressed myself against the sergeant's leg.

"It's all right, Darling." He gave me a reassuring pat on the head. "They'll calm down. And you'll be kenneled behind the barracks with the other ladies."

The sergeant led me around a squat building where there were only five wooden boxes. Two were empty. Three held other females: a sleek tan racer, a squat spaniel, and a sad-eyed Airedale. None barked. Instead they all stared at Sergeant Hanson, their tails wagging hopefully.

"Private Kent will bring dinner soon, lasses," he said as he steered me to the last crate. "This is Darling. She'll be your new mate."

I raised my lip and showed my teeth when the three looked at me. *No, I will not be your mate. Rags is my only friend. And I will be away from this place as soon as I get loose.*

I felt the sergeant's fingers on my collar as he took off the leash and tied on a rope. He tested the knot, then straightened. Immediately, I lunged to the end of the line.

"Aye, Darling. Your Robert and Katherine wrote that you like to run away. Only there will be none of that here." Sergeant Hanson looked down at me, his hands on his hips. I bit at the rope, but it was thick and tough.

"You belong to the British Army now," he went on. "You are no longer a pet, nor is your name Darling. You are War Dog 204. This will be your home for the next six weeks, and when you leave here, it'll be on a steamer to France—and to war."

## CHAPTER 5

# War Dog 204

Beginning of April 1917

**N**ight. Dark and starless. The lorry rumbled up the road and then slowed on a desolate strip of beach. Sergeant Hanson stood in the open-air back of the truck and I stood with him. The handlers sat on benches along the sides, their dogs in front of them.

"This will be the first real test for the dogs," Sergeant Hanson said, swaying with the truck's movement. "Messenger dogs have proved themselves to be four to five times faster than a man when delivering dispatches in war areas. Let's see how this group does."

I recognized the hound called Beast, and Tweed, the sad-eyed Airedale. The others were unknown to me. After three weeks of learning commands—sit, stay, heel, retrieve, down, begone—I no longer snarled at strange dogs. I no longer strained at my rope. But my thoughts were still on Katherine and Robert and my family back home, and I hoped that tonight I would get my chance to run away.

"Their keepers are back at the kennels, waiting for us to release the dogs," the sergeant continued. "We'll see which one makes it back in record time."

"And who gets lost in the mudflats," one of the handlers added.

"And 'oo ends up in Shoeburyness begging at the butcher's," another chimed in. Everyone laughed.

Sergeant Hanson didn't even smile. "Messenger dogs must feel a keen delight in carrying out their duties. Tonight will determine which ones will continue training—and which will be destroyed."

The laughter died down.

Tweed whimpered. She pined for her cozy bed by the fire as much as I pined for my children and freedom.

"No torches are allowed to light the way, so tread carefully through the marsh. We'll spread out. Smythe, McCann, and Reeves—head west up the beach. Harlow, Jasper, and Donnelly—head east. When I blow the whistle, release your dog with the command 'begone.'"

We jumped from the lorry, and the other men and dogs silently disappeared into the night. I trotted down the beach by Sergeant Hanson's side. He was silent too. I had grown numb to the constant barking of dogs and orders, so this quiet night was a treat. It reminded me of many nights in Cosham. After the family was in bed, I would wiggle under the picket fence and join Rags. We would explore the village, tipping over rubbish bins and lunging at stray cats.

What had happened to my old pal? Had Constable George finally caught him? Or worse, had he been shot? My heart saddened at the thought. But soon I would be back in Cosham to find the answer. And when I returned, I would sneak bones to Rags every day. And I wouldn't run away from my family ever again.

Sergeant Hanson turned off the beach and into the mudflats. My paws sunk deep, and spiny marsh grasses snagged my fur. We wound past fallen branches and gnarled stumps. I heard the shrill *whoo-whoo* of the train whistle in the distance. I turned my head toward the sound. How long would it take me to reach Cosham from here?

"Darling." A firm tug on the leash got my attention. Sergeant Hanson kneeled in the mud in front of me. His eyes were solemn as he held my furry head in his hands. "This is the last test for you. You are smart and swift. You have learned every command faster than any dog at the school. You would be a fine messenger but alas, your heart is not in it. You are too lightweight for pulling artillery and too shy for sentry duty. The major has identified you as a dog he expects to fail tonight. And if you do"—his voice caught—

"you will not return to Robert and Katherine."

He removed my collar and slid a different one around my neck. This one had a metal canister attached to it. I knew what the special collar meant: "return to my keeper."

"Private Kent is waiting for you and your message. He has liver treats and a bowl of cool water," Sergeant Hanson told me. "Now it is up to you." Unhooking the leash, he stepped back, gave the whistle one shrill blow, and ordered. "Begone."

I took off, running toward the sound of the train whistle. This was the first time I had been turned loose so far from the kennels and the first time I had drilled at night. No one would see me if I ran away. If I raced swiftly, I should reach Cosham by sunup.

A loud crash from the beach made me whirl. Beast lunged through the tall grass, passing me without a glance as he headed for the kennels. I paused, watching him go. My thoughts went to Private Kent, who fed me morning and night, brushed my fur, and cleaned my crate—all with a gentle pat and kind words.

My thoughts turned back to Robert and Katherine. I remembered racing free through the village with Rags. The canister and "return" meant nothing to me. Once again I started for the railway.

Then my ears picked up a cry. I stopped in my tracks. It was Sergeant Hanson. I would recognize his voice anywhere. The cry came again, and this time I heard his distress.

Without a second thought, I plunged back the way I had come. I found him sitting up, half hidden in the grass. One leg was stretched in front of him at an odd angle. His face was pale. "Aye, Darling, it's you. I'm glad you came back, but I was hoping one of the men would hear me. It looks like I've gone and twisted my leg falling over this wretched stump in the dark."

I didn't need him to say any more. I didn't need to hear "begone" or "return." The pain in his face told me everything.

I licked his hand where it clutched his knee and then raced for the kennels and Private Kent.

Between the beach and barracks were many obstacles. We had practiced leaping ditches and gates and crawling through barbed wire and tunnels. Once I made it through the marsh, I came upon some scruffy bushes and a pen. *Goats!* My nose twitched at their pungent smell. One stamped the ground and shook his horns when I peered through the slatted fence.

*Herd them, chase them,* rang in my head. But this time I couldn't. I had to ignore my instincts and get help for Sergeant Hanson.

On the other side of the goat pen was a forest of sea-wind stunted trees. Once through it, I would find the barracks and Private Kent. The yellow glow of a lantern spurred me onward.

Private Kent's face lit up when he saw me. I saw no sign of Beast, Tweed, or the other dogs.

"Good girl," he praised. "I knew you could do it. Even though the other dogs came in long before you," he added, sounding gloomy. He reached for my collar, but I danced out of his way. His brows lowered. "Come 'ere, Darling. I 'ave your liver treat."

I didn't want liver. I wanted Private Kent to follow me. I knew not to bark. "Silent" had been drilled into us from the beginning. So I twirled around and I dashed back toward the woods.

"Darling." His voice was firmer this time. "*Come!*"

Just then Private Carlton walked up with Beast. "I do believe Beast was first," the handler said with proud smile. "And Darling last. And now she's playing a game of chase?"

"I don't know what's gotten into 'er," Private Kent said.

Just then the lorry rumbled down the lane. The handlers jumped out. "Is Sergeant Hanson back?" the driver called out the open window.

Private Kent strode up. "Wasn't 'e supposed to return with you?"

"We couldn't find him. We thought he might have walked cross country for some reason."

Private Kent's eyes widened under his cap as he looked down at me. "So that's what you're trying to tell me, eh, girl? Something's 'appened to the sergeant?"

This time I obeyed when he called me into the back of the lorry along with two other men. The canister and its message were forgotten. When we reached the beach, I jumped out before the truck stopped. I dashed off, following Sergeant Hanson's and my scents.

"Slow down," Private Kent struggled to keep up with me. Darting left, I headed into the marsh.

"Over here." Sergeant Hanson's cry was soft, but my keen ears easily heard it. When I reached him, I nuzzled him and he smiled weakly. His face was white, his breathing shallow. The sound of rustling and thrashing from the direction of the beach told me that Private Kent was not far behind. Still, I didn't bark. I left Sergeant Hanson for a brief moment to alert Private Kent to where we were, and then went back to the sergeant.

"Found 'im!" Kent hollered. Quickly he bent and felt Sergeant Hanson's pulse. "Looks like you're going into shock. Glad we got 'ere when we did."

"Leg's all messed up." Sergeant Hanson tried to

smile as he struggled to sit up. "I didn't follow my own orders to tread carefully."

"Save your strength," Private Kent told him. "Private Jeeves 'as a medical kit. We'll get a Tommy splint on that leg and get you out of 'ere. Might not be broken, right?"

I lay down beside Sergeant Hanson, warming his chilled body. All thoughts of Cosham had flown from my head.

"Darling 'ere brought us," Private Kent said. "She's no messenger dog, that's a fact. She came in dead last. But might it be she 'as a different calling?" He slipped off his tunic and laid it across Sergeant Hanson's chest. "I've heard they're training mercy dogs. Dogs that 'elp find the wounded. What do you think of that? Sergeant?" He patted the man's cheeks as if he were a dog. "Stay awake, now. Don't want you losing consciousness."

I looked up as the others arrived. Private Jeeves slipped his pack from his back as he walked. Another soldier carried a stretcher under his arm.

"Darling'll wear a red cross on her jacket and 'elp soldiers at the Front," Kent continued as Private Jeeves kneeled and opened the bag, "just like she 'elped you, right Sergeant? And I'd be proud to train 'er."

"As I would…" Sergeant Hanson's voice trailed off and his eyes drifted shut. His fingers laced themselves in my ruff. He didn't let go, and I didn't leave his side until he was safely on the stretcher.

## CHAPTER 6

# A New Mission

End of April 1917

*oom!* Dirt blew skyward right in front of me. I scooted around the blast, intent on my mission: *Find the wounded.*

*Boom!* A second blast ripped the earth, and rocks rained on my head like hail. I sank into a ditch, waited, ran again. Ahead I saw a soldier's helmet above the tall beach grass, and then a muddy boot and khaki-colored trouser leg.

I nosed the leg, feeling for warmth. "Good girl, 204," the soldier murmured when I got within his reach. He removed a canteen of water from the saddlebags strapped to my back and took a sip. When he was done, I raced back the way I had come.

Coils of barbed wire blocked my way, but I leaped over them without hesitation. Suddenly the *rat-a-tat-tat* of a machine gun sounded in front of me. I crouched, making myself small, and crawled into a ditch. When all was quiet, I dashed toward a stone fence. I jumped the fence and then zigzagged across the last stretch. Leaping into a trench, I landed at Private Kent's feet.

"It's 204," someone said behind me. "The first dog to report back."

Immediately I lay down. That was the signal that I had found a wounded soldier. Private Kent clipped on my leash.

Sergeant Hanson stood behind him. He was propped on crutches, his trouser leg torn to reveal a white cast from ankle to knee. "That's *Darling*," he said in a low voice. I could hear his pride.

Private Kent lifted me up and set me on the parapet, the top edge of the trench. I waited while he climbed the ladder. Then I led the way as he and two stretcher bearers and an orderly followed. The trip I had made in minutes seemed to take them forever. Private Kent had to cut the barbed wire I had leaped over. Several times we flattened ourselves to the ground as the zing of gunfire filled the air. But I didn't flag in my purpose: *find the wounded soldier.*

Finally I saw him. Straining at the leash, I pulled Private Kent forward. The soldier pretending to be wounded grinned. "She passed this drill with flying colors, eh, Private Kent?"

He nodded. "Neither bombs nor gunfire stopped 'er. It were a good thing we switched her training from a messenger dog to a mercy dog." Even the stretcher bearers were grinning at me as they helped the "wounded" man to his feet. Pleased, I sat back on my haunches and begged as if at the butcher shop. But this time it wasn't for bones. It was for praise. I knew that I had done something special during this practice.

The orderly shrugged on his pack and patted my head.

"Don't fuss over 'er too much," Private Kent warned. "Mercy dogs aren't pets." His voice was firm, but he was still smiling as he gave me a treat of liver. "Sergeant Hanson'll be pleased. A bit sweet on this one, 'e is. Plans on taking 'er to France himself as soon as 'is leg is mended." He puffed out his chest proudly. "The sergeant's been assigned to the sectional kennels at the front lines in Belgium. I'm going with 'im."

"By then the war may be over," the orderly said. "Now that the Americans have joined the fight."

The soldier who'd played the role of a wounded man snorted loudly as he lay down on the canvas stretcher. "About time. America declared war on the Germans in April. Where've their troops been all this time?"

"The British had to lose thousands more soldiers before bloody Wilson would send his precious army to Europe," the orderly said bitterly.

"France and the other allies have lost too many men as well," the soldier on the stretcher said. "Don't you add to the numbers when you're over there, Private Kent."

"I plan on keepin' me 'ead away from those German bullets," Private Kent replied. "But 204 'ere won't be so lucky. She'll be searching for wounded in no man's land."

All four swung their gazes to me, and their faces were no longer smiling. "So let's 'ope the war's over soon," he added softly as he stroked my head, "or this lass will be one more casualty."

**CHAPTER 7**

# From England to Belgium

Mid-May 1917

The road was muddy beneath my paws, the sky overcast. Silence surrounded us as we walked through what was once a village like Cosham. The shops and houses were gone. All that stood were chimneys jutting into the sky like leafless trees and jagged brick walls and skeletal frames that held no roofs.

There was a small herd of us—handlers and dogs. We had traveled by boat across the English Channel and landed in a place Private Kent had called "France." From there we rode by railway and lorry into the countryside.

Once across the border into the place called "Belgium," we walked, except for Sergeant Hanson, who rode in a motorbike sidecar. The railcars and lorries were packed with ammunition and troops heading to the Front, and there was no room for dogs.

At first I was happy to be walking. The air ruffled my fur and filled my nose with new scents. But soon the view grew stark despite the full flush of spring. Trees were broken in half, craters of mud pocked the farmland, and the smell of burned wood was strong.

A few people poked through the ruins of the village, looking for something they could salvage. Their faces were dirty and forlorn and their stares unwelcoming. A cart piled high with people and belongings rumbled past, pulled by one skinny horse. I paused when I saw the faces of two children peering from the top. I wagged my tail in greeting, but they didn't smile as they passed us by. Then the sharp crack of the whip over the cob's back made me shy away.

"Refugees headed to France," Private Carlton said. He stood beside us with Beast, who had passed his messenger dog training with flying colors. Private Reeves held Tweed's leash. Like me, she'd been trained as a mercy dog.

Except for the rumble of engines and tromp of boots, the village was silent. Finally Private Kent spoke. "No wonder the Belgians aren't friendly. They didn't ask for this war. The Germans just invaded and took over. And now 'ere *we* are."

Private Reeves snorted. "We need to be here, invited or not. We have to push the Huns clear out of Belgium before there's nothing left of the country."

Sergeant Hanson signaled us to stop and rest in the shade of a wall. A line of horse-drawn wagons and trucks, both loaded with supplies, snaked past us. Private Kent pulled off his haversack. He pulled out his tin cup and took his canteen from his cartridge belt. After pouring me some water, he fed me a sliver of dried liver. Then he had his own snack of bully beef and crackers.

Sergeant Hanson ruffled my fur and slipped me a treat, too. His brace was off but he still favored his leg.

"We're nearing Messines," he said to the group. "Once we're at headquarters, there will be no rest. We've been assigned to the 10th Battalion Worcestershire Regiment."

Murmurs of approval went around. "Mates from close to me 'ome," one handler said.

"The soldiers have been building up trenches and laying tracks. More supplies are needed for a major attack under General Plumer," Sergeant Hanson continued. "The Allies are planning on taking Messines Ridge from the Germans."

"And we want to be part of it," another handler said.

"Then let's continue. The main camp is five miles farther. That's where headquarters and the dog kennel are."

We marched on, and soon the silence was shattered. A group of planes soared overhead like migrating geese. I heard the *rat-a-tat-tat* of machine-gun fire in the distance, followed by louder blasts that I knew were bombs—like the ones used in our training.

Our pace picked up and I could feel the tension in Private Kent's grip on my leash.

From behind us came a rattling and roaring as I'd never heard before. Private Kent stopped and turned. "Well, I'll be a kippered 'erring. Never thought I'd lay eyes on a tank, and 'ere are a dozen coming right at us."

"Those are the new Mark IVs," Private Reeves said. He whistled in amazement as Tweed cowered behind his legs. "Easy lass. They're on our side."

Everyone stepped back and Sergeant Hanson's driver pulled off the road. As the tanks passed, the handlers cheered. I growled, upset by the giant rolling things and their deafening noise. A man poked his head from the top and saluted. His face was totally covered by a helmet and visor.

The handlers saluted back. "We should've had a tank at the War Dog School," Private Carlton said. "To get the dogs used to the sight."

Unafraid, Beast lunged for a clanking track as it rolled past, churning up the earth.

"The dogs will soon be seeing things that no one can train them for." Sergeant Hanson frowned. "Let's hope they stay true."

As we moved along, the road and roadsides became even more crowded. Men unloaded huge howitzer shells from railway cars onto wagon beds. Mules carried boxes of ammunition in packs on their backs. Shirtless soldiers lifted rocks and sandbags into truck beds. Two dogs hauled a cart loaded with buckets of water for the workers. The dogs had once been hand-some mastiffs, but now their coats were dull and their ribs showed. They reminded me of Cosham strays—and Rags.

All the while gunfire boomed in the distance and smoke billowed in the air.

We slowed to let a ragged group of soldiers march wearily past us, heading in the direction we had come. Some had bandages around their eyes and were guided by their comrades. Behind them, soldiers pushed hand carts holding unconscious men, draped inside like sacks of grain.

"Looks like those lads were hit by poison gas." I felt Private Kent shudder. I knew the word "gas." We had practiced wearing our masks at the War Dog School. Though they said it would protect me, I hated the way it felt around my muzzle.

A familiar cooing noise made me glance sharply to the left. Four soldiers walked briskly alongside the road. On their backs were square baskets with lids.

They were full of birds. *Pigeons!*

I hadn't seen a pigeon since we'd left France. Now here were baskets of them. What were the pesky birds doing here? Several fluttered their wings, and I heard more cooing. I began to dance in place. Maybe war would be fun after all.

"Settle down, girl," Private Kent said. "Those pigeons aren't to chase. They carry messages, like Beast. We're almost there, thank the Queen," he added. "Me boots are rubbing me 'eels raw."

Soon we arrived "there"—a farmhouse surrounded by sheds, a barn, and rows and rows of tents, large and small.

Sergeant Hanson climbed from the sidecar. "Head-quarters," he said. "The kennels are on the far side of the barn."

Headquarters was almost like a village. We passed a bakery in a tent, where workers were loading loaves into the wagons. A team of horses pulled a second wagon, already loaded, toward the fighting. I hoped that somewhere there was a wagon full of beef bones.

"The largest tent houses the Advanced Dressing Station for the wounded," Sergeant Hanson explained. "First they are treated at Regimental Aid Posts at the Front. They then come here or go to Field Ambulances far behind the line. Severe cases are sent on to general hospitals."

As we passed by the tent, I smelled blood and antiseptic. I had been taught to recognize those scents, to find warmth and a pulse, and then to lead my handler to the wounded soldier. The orderlies and stretcher bearers would follow us, carrying the medicine and bandages.

Under a lone tree beside the barn, horses were picketed to a line. Nosebags hung from their heads. Like the mastiffs, they were skinny and worn, and many lay in the straw as if exhausted.

Finally we came to the kennels. Slatted crates stood in two rows. Dogs were tied to some; others were empty. Unlike the dogs at the War School, these did not bark or leap. They were curled in front on dusty blankets and barely looked our way.

A soldier, his uniform marked like Sergeant Hanson's came up to us. "I'm Sergeant Cary-Hough," he said. "Good to see you. We are in need of a fresh dog squad."

"We have twenty dogs and twenty handlers," Sergeant Hanson said. "All are ready to work."

Sergeant Cary-Hough nodded as if pleased. "The dogs have been invaluable here as messengers, scouts, and sentries. Initially the generals and the troops were skeptical, but the animals proved themselves time and time again. The Germans have kept up constant firing against us all month. There have been many casualties, and this dog squad has worked valiantly and is slated to be relieved."

"And the dogs that aren't here?" Private Kent eyed the crates, many of which were empty. "They're still at the Front?"

Sergeant Cary-Hough shook his head. "Alas, only one in four messenger dogs makes it through. Horses, soldiers, dogs, pigeons—none are spared. We have a small veterinary corps housed behind the line, but they are overworked, as we all are."

Private Kent reached down and stroked my head as the sergeant continued to talk.

"Each dog is assigned a crate. The numbers are nailed to the front. Rest tonight. Tomorrow, the 10th Regiment will be heading forward to the trenches near Wytschaete. You will go with them. On June 7, we will attack Messines Ridge in force. The Germans have had a stronghold on the ridge since 1914. If we are to be victorious, there is much to be done beforehand."

Sergeant Cary-Hough led the handlers and dogs toward the crates. Private Kent removed my leash and tied me to a crate with a rope. "The tag on top says 204," he muttered. "That should say 'Darling,' right, girl?"

I wagged my tail. He left after saying my favorite word—dinner—and I began to sniff my new home.

*Home.* Faded images of Robert, Katherine, Mum, Father, and Baby filled my head. I thought of my cozy basket by the kitchen cooker and the nest I made on Katherine's quilt when Mum wasn't looking. I thought of playing in the streets of Cosham with Rags and begging for bones at the butchers.

Now home was a straw bed, a patch of dirt, and a bowl in front of a wooden crate. And worse, I could smell the dog that had lived there before me. I was not fearless like Beast, nor cowardly like Tweed. But somehow I knew that the dog that had lived in this home before me was no longer alive—and it made me tremble.

**CHAPTER 8**

# The Trenches

May 20, 1917

The stench hit me as I followed Private Kent down the trench. Sweat. Dirt. Feet. Rotten flesh. Rats. *Fear.* With my sense of smell, one hundred times stronger than a human's, I could sniff out the lice hidden in the seams of uniforms and strands of hair.

Soldiers filed along the trenches—earthen lanes that twisted to the right and left of us. The sun glinted on their green helmets, making me think of the beetles that scurried about in the fissures of the chalk mines at home.

From headquarters, I had followed Private Kent, Private Carlton and Beast, and six other dogs and handlers. Sergeant Cary-Hough escorted us down the communication trench, then through support trenches filled with supplies and leading to the front line. In some places we walked on wood duckboards. Other places we slogged through mud. When we were close to the Front, the sergeant introduced us to the Battalion Medical Officer. Wounded soldiers would first be carried to him at the RAP, or Regimental Aid Post, a fancy name for a space with a plank floor and dirt walls and roof, outfitted with two bunks and a few medical supplies.

Finally we reached the front line—the trench closest to the enemy. The other dogs and handlers turned south. "We're headed north toward Wytschaete and the Germans," Sergeant Cary-Hough said.

Ladders led into and out of the trenches on the sides facing the fighting. The walls were reinforced with logs and sandbags. The soldiers on guard duty

stood tall, the barrels of their rifles resting on the parapet. Occasionally, one would shoot a volley in the direction of the German line. Enemy gunfire constantly zinged overhead.

The soldiers who weren't on duty reached out to pat me, their fingers grimy with gunpowder and dirt. Some stood, eating from their mess kits. Others wrote letters, cleaned guns, or polished boots. Most napped, propped up against trench walls or boxes of ammunition.

Finally, we reported to Second Lieutenant Luckman of the 10th Worcestershire Regiment.

"Pleased to see fresh dogs," he said. "Let's hope we won't need them. As soon as it's dark, two parties of hand-picked soldiers are raiding a German bunker."

I could feel Private Kent's anticipation. Beside me, Beast quivered, as if ready to leap from the trench and take a message back to headquarters. I wasn't quite as excited about being so near the shooting. Thoughts of the war dogs who hadn't returned stayed with me.

"Dog 204 will wait with the medical corps in the dugout." The second lieutenant pointed to wooden stairs leading into the dark. "And 203 will come with the raiding party."

"The Beast and I are ready for action," Private Carlton said. Private Kent seemed just as happy to lead me down the few steps further into the dank earth.

Cigarette smoke filled the small underground room.

Inside stood two men wearing armbands marked with a red cross and an SB for stretcher bearer, and an orderly who also wore a red cross. They nodded. "I'm Robert," one of the stretcher bearers said. "Welcome to the Front."

I took notice when I heard the name. I thought of my Robert and Katherine. Would I see them ever again?

"Where waiting feels like eternity," the orderly added.

"And the biscuits are hard as rocks," the second stretcher bearer said, trying to bite into one. "I'm Private Thacker. That's Churchill." He nodded at the orderly. "And Sir Robert there introduced himself like the gent he is."

"We're glad to see a Red Cross dog," Churchill said. "No man's land is pitted with craters, bunkers, and abandoned funk 'oles. It's easy to lose the wounded. The last dog 'elped us bring back every last one."

I was glad that Private Kent didn't ask what had happened to the last dog. Instead he ruffled my ears reassuringly and said, "Darling—204—is the best."

Robert sighed. "*Darling.* That's how I start my letters back home to my sweetheart." Leaning forward, he stroked my head. "Will you be the good luck I need to get back to England and the girl I love?"

"That's all the lad talks about," Thacker said. "Me, I've got a wife and a passel of kids. My army wages keep the lot from starving."

"When they pays us," Churchill grunted.

Thacker cuffed him. "Quit grumblin'. At least you're not some poor infantry bloke racing across no man's land in the pitch dark. Unless a shell or bomb hits this dugout, we're safe."

"And thank the Queen the mud's dried," Robert said. "Last skirmish it took four of us to move one wounded man to safety. Sunk in to our knees, we did. Made perfect targets. The blasted Huns don't care if you have a red cross on your arm or not."

I shivered. Private Kent made me lie down beside his leg. Pulling a piece of dried liver from his pocket, he fed it to me. I was glad for my handler. No matter what the situation, he always looked out for me.

For what seemed like forever, we waited in the dim hole. Water dripped from the roof. A rat scurried in the corner. Finally, I put my head down and closed my eyes, trying to shut out the noise, the smell, the rats—and the worry.

Private Kent woke me with an urgent tug on my leash. I jumped to my feet and followed him up the stairs. It was night, starlit and bright. Soldiers lined the trench as far to the right as I could see. Their faces were solemn. To the left was the very end of the trench. Beast and Private Carlton stood there, waiting for orders. Second Lieutenant Luckman strode behind the small group of soldiers on the right, giving words of encouragement. Then he lifted his rifle and climbed the ladder. "Over the top, lads," he ordered briskly. "We're headed to Nag's Nose. Let's get those Germans."

All along the trench, soldiers scrambled up the ladders, stepped over the parapet, and disappeared into the night. I strained at the end of the leash, wanting to climb with them, wanting to see what was happening. Private Carlton and an infantry soldier lifted Beast to the top of the parapet. The big hound bristled with excitement as the infantryman took his leash and hurried up the ladder after him. Private Carlton stayed in the trench. If a message needed to be sent from the small raiding party, Beast would carry it back to his handler.

I stayed behind with Privates Kent and Carlton, the orderly, and the stretcher bearers. A small reserve troop from the 10th remained as well. They manned the trench, their rifles pointed in the direction the raiding party had gone, ready to act as reinforcements if needed.

All was silent. Then shots rang out. A volley of machine-gun fire ripped through the night. I jumped at the deafening blast of a bomb. Then silence again.

Had Beast and the others made it across no man's land? Would there be wounded for me to find? There was no way to know what was happening, and all of us in the trench held our breaths, waiting.

Just when I thought I could wait no longer, we heard a shout. Private Kent climbed the ladder and poked his head over the top of the parapet.

"It's our boys! All of 'em!" he called down after counting out loud. "Didn't lose a man. Wait, there's more coming back than left. Well, I'll be a plum pudding! They've brought prisoners with 'em."

I whined softly, wanting to see. Private Kent lifted me to the top. I looked from one soldier to the next, finally spotting Beast strutting beside Private Carlton.

"Fine job, Tommies!" a reserve soldier shouted. The men of the raiding party whooped in return. I danced on the parapet, greeting them. Smiles stretched their grimy faces under their helmets.

Suddenly the *rat-a-tat-tat* of a machine gun made them flatten to the ground. They crawled the rest of the way, then hurried down the ladder, eager to tell the story of the raid.

"Surprised eight Germans, hiding in a bunker."

"The 33rd Fusiliers."

"Bayoneted six. They died without a peep."

"Bet they wish they'd never met a Tommy."

"Two surrendered." The last soldier nodded toward the two men in gray uniforms who stood with their heads hanging. "Lucky for them they did, or they'd be dead, too."

Second Lieutenant Luckman was the last to climb down the ladder into the safety of the trench. "Excellent job," he told his men. "That's the proper way to win the war. No mucking about." Then he turned to the two German soldiers. "Take these prisoners back to headquarters."

Private Kent kneeled beside me. "Take a good look, lass," he said. "There's the enemy."

I stared at the prisoners, wanting to growl. But then I saw how worn and dazed they looked. And when I studied their faces, I saw that the two hated Germans were just boys, not much older than Robert.

## CHAPTER 9

# "Begone"

June 2, 1917

For a week, we'd been waiting at headquarters— drilling for the day when we would be in service. We were assigned to the 3$^{rd}$ Battalion Worcestershire, B Company. Twice we had been sent to the Front, but we hadn't been called into action on either trip.

Tweed, however, had seen plenty of action during her mission. Private Reeves gave glowing accounts of how she had bravely led the orderlies to the wounded. I could sense Tweed's new confidence. Still, when she'd returned to the kennel, she'd slept as if exhausted. Even a filled dinner bowl wouldn't rouse her.

When we were called to the Front again, Sergeant Hanson accompanied us. He was in charge of our group of six dogs and handlers. As we made our way down a muddy trench, a small brown dog hurtled past me. He dove beneath a crate of ammunition and I heard the *snap* of his jaws. The noise startled me. Rags had killed rats with a *snap* just like that.

The dog emerged, his prey hanging limp from his mouth. I let out a yelp of joy. It *was* Rags!

Instantly, he dropped the dead rat and sprang on top of me. Wrestling and chewing, we greeted each other while Sergeant Hanson and Private Kent stared in wonder.

"Why, she knows that mutt!" Private Kent said.

"That's our mascot," one of the soldiers in B Company said.

Several of his buddies gathered round. "Private Rags," another man added.

"Keeps this place clean of mice and rats."

One of them pointed to lines scratched in the dirt wall. "Sure enough, 'e's up to a hundred."

"Best soldier in our company. Came from the Battersea Dogs Home."

"Now he's got a home with us."

Rags left me and ran from soldier to soldier. Each man patted and praised him. I wiggled with delight. Now I could stop worrying about my friend. He finally had a family.

"Time to say your farewells now, Darling," Private Kent said. "Come."

Rags and I tussled one last time. Picking up the rat, he held it proudly in his mouth. That was the picture I kept in my mind as I trotted down the trench again. Rags had his job in the army, and so did I.

Once we were at the jumping-off point, we met Lieutenant Hudson, commander of the new company. He gave everyone their orders. "Our target is the German communication line we call Nutmeg Avenue and a supply line named Nutmeg Support. Wire cutters have been sent ahead. When it's dark, we'll go over the parapet and lay down in the open. We'll listen for the British artillery to let loose, and then we'll dash forward and bomb the lines."

Again Private Kent and I waited in a dugout with the men from the medical corp. He checked his equipment, then refolded the bandages in my saddlebags. An orderly heated water from his canteen to make tea. A stretcher bearer wrote something on the back of sardine tin label. "Want to hear my poem?" he asked when he was finished.

No one replied, but he read it aloud anyway.

*Thirty days the earth was blasted,*
*and the British Tommies fell.*
*Thirty nights we dared not rest.*
*We waited for the shell*
*that signaled our comrades' deaths.*

"Don't rhyme proper," the orderly said.

"'Fell' and 'shell' do," the stretcher bearer protested.

"Where's mention of the bloody rations?" the other stretcher bearer complained. "If I eat one more tin of cold bully beef, I'll mutiny."

"I thought your poem were right powerful," Private Kent said solemnly.

"Thank you, mate." Folding the paper, the stretcher bearer slipped it in his pocket. "If I die, you can send it to the *Wipers Times.*"

"The *Wipers Times?*" Private Kent asked.

"You haven't heard of our trench magazine?" The orderly pulled another folded paper from his pocket. "Named after the town of Ypres, which us stupid Brits call Wipers 'cause we can't pronounce the Belgian name. The mag's filled with good old English humor." He opened the magazine. "Listen to today's weather report. 'From five to one—mist. From eleven to two—east wind. From eight to one—chlorine gas.'"

Laughter rose in the small earthen room, and as the orderly continued to read aloud, I dozed, comforted by the cheerful voices.

At dark, Sergeant Hanson roused us. We hurried up the steps from the dugout to the trench. Sensing the tension when we emerged, I stayed close by Private Kent's side.

Lieutenant Hudson was inspecting his men, who stood tall and ready despite their weary stares and dirt-streaked uniforms. I scanned their faces. Some were as young as the German soldiers who had been taken prisoner. Others looked as if they'd been fighting forever.

"It's time," the lieutenant finally said. "Let's mop them up." With that, Company B streamed over the top.

Private Kent and I, Private Reeves and Tweed, and a messenger dog and his handler stayed behind. Sergeant Hanson went with Company B and the remaining handlers and dogs.

Almost immediately, a barrage of heavy British artillery split the air. "Right on schedule," Private Kent said. "Company B should be nearing its target." I pictured the soldiers running forward in the dark. The Germans firing blindly. Soldiers on both sides falling.

The whine of an incoming shell made me cringe.

"Gas!" The sentries' warning cries rang up and down the trench. Private Kent didn't need to hear the word twice. He yanked his mask over his head, then reached in his canvas bag for mine. Quickly, he buckled it on me. I hated that mask. I could barely see out and it pinched my muzzle. But when I saw a soldier clutch his throat because he had been too slow to obey the warning, I was glad Private Kent had reacted swiftly.

Bombs continued to rend the air. Suddenly a horrendous *boom* crashed near us. Above and beyond the trench, earth rose in the air as high as Portsdown Hill.

"The Huns are blowing up the howitzer battery!" someone hollered. Private Kent covered me with his body as dirt and metal rained over us. When he straightened, there was blood on his cheek. I nuzzled my head against him. "Just a nick, lass," he assured me.

Finally a breeze carried the gas fumes away, and the sentries' all-clear cry ran up and down the trench. Slowly, men began to take off their masks. Private Kent unbuckled mine but kept it ready by his side. Only one soldier seemed sick; an orderly quickly led him away.

Flares rose from the German front, lighting the dark. "They know something's up," Private Kent whispered. Minutes later, the shrieks of incoming shells and the thuds of bombs hitting the ground reached my ears. The earth shook. Again, I heard the rapid fire of a machine gun. I was used to these sounds, but this time they seemed closer. My heart beat faster and I huddled closer to Private Kent.

As silently as they had left, B Company returned with twelve prisoners. I spotted Sergeant Hanson and Private Carlton, who supported a limping British soldier between them. Blood stained the leg of the man's trouser. Beast trailed behind.

I hopped up and greeted them with wagging tail. Sergeant Hanson leaned down and held me for a second. His face was grave. "Soon it'll be your turn to prove yourself, Darling," he said.

"We cleared the walking wounded," Lieutenant Hudson told the medical corps. "But without torches to light the way, we had to leave behind those too injured to call out. It's up to you and the dogs to find them."

All eyes turned to Tweed and me.

For a brief moment, terror rippled down my spine.

Then I spun toward the ladder—this was what I had been trained for.

Without hesitation, Private Kent and Sergeant Hanson lifted me to the top of the parapet. "Begone," Sergeant Hanson said, a tremor in his voice that only I could hear.

Then Private Kent unsnapped my leash, and I raced into the black night.

A flare ripped through the sky and for an instant I could see the ghostly stretch of land before me. It was riddled with holes and heaped with stones, earth, and shrapnel.

I ran, slowing when I saw the glint of wire. We'd been taught to leap over, crawl under, or go around the sharp barbs that caught fur and tore skin.

Spotting a dark shape draped over the wire, I belly-crawled to it. When I pressed my nose against a hand, there was no sign of life. Quickly, I found a break in the coils made by the wire cutters and moved on. I was in no man's land.

I lifted my head and sniffed the air. Among the smells of spent artillery and disturbed earth, I detected a different scent. *There…to my right.* My eyesight was keen, but the shadows made by the looming mounds and twisted trunks confused me. Airplane engines roared overhead. Gunfire strafed the ground in the direction of our front line. The Germans were fighting back.

There was no time to lose. My senses told me there was a wounded soldier nearby, trapped in no man's land, and I had to find him.

## CHAPTER 10

# No Man's Land

June 2, 1917

Where was the wounded soldier? Had he fallen in a hole? Had he pulled himself to safety behind a pile of rocks?

Hoping to pick up a trail, I kept my nose to the ground. The smells of burnt earth, gunpowder, and a hundred boot soles grew confusing. I lifted my head and zigzagged back and forth at a trot. Whenever there was a moment's silence, I stopped to listen.

Blasts made the sky glow. Then a searchlight shone upward on a German observation balloon. The light reflected onto the ground and I spotted a figure sitting against a tree that had been cut in half by shells.

I ran over. The soldier was slumped sideways, barely breathing. I recognized one of the young men from Company B. When I nosed his palm, it was cold, but there was a faint flutter at his wrist. He was alive.

I pawed his arm, hoping to rouse him. My saddlebags held water and bandages. But this soldier needed more help than I could give.

I nuzzled his hand one last time, hoping he would understand that I had found him—and that I would return.

Leaving him, I raced in a straight line for the barbed wire and dove through the same opening I'd used before. I didn't need to follow my tracks. I knew the fastest way to the trench.

Then a shell whistled overhead. *Boom!* The impact split the earth. Dirt and shrapnel blew me into the air. I landed hard on my side. Stunned, I lay panting. Raining earth covered me like a coat.

"Darling. Come 'ere, girl." Private Kent was crawling on his belly toward me. I lifted my head at the sound of his voice. "Are you all right?" He brushed the dirt off me and I struggled upright. "We're thirty yards away."

Standing, I shook off the rest of the dirt. My ribs ached but I had a job to do—a soldier to save. Quickly, I lay back down.

"You found 'im, didn't you? Stretcher bearers, double-time!" he called hoarsely. The bearers scrambled over the parapet.

Private Kent clipped the leash to my collar. We set off again, leading the way through the dark. The wire cutter reached the barbed coils right after we did. Snipping and yanking, he cleared a new path. Then he beckoned us onward.

I rushed ahead, tugging at the leash. Often we had to stop and wait for the men from the medical corps. Smoke from the bombs hung like fog, and the soldiers could not light their way with torches lest they draw the Germans' attention. The orderly stumbled into a shell hole and had to be pulled out. Private Kent tripped over a root and fell to his knees. I whined encouragement. *Hurry, hurry.*

Gunfire ripped past us. We all hit the ground and froze.

"We must be near the German front," the orderly whispered, fear making his voice quiver.

Private Kent nodded. Using his arms to pull himself forward, he wormed behind a pile of rubble. The stretcher bearers crawled after him, dragging the rolled-up stretcher. Last came the wire cutter and the orderly, panting like a dog. The five exhausted men leaned against the rubble and waited for the firing to stop.

No man's land was treacherous.

After a moment's silence, I leaped up again. Beyond the pile, I spotted the jagged tree. I wanted to bark *There! Over there!* But my training had taught me that enemy rifles would aim at any sound.

Instead, when Private Kent stood again, I crouched down and then darted madly toward the tree, pulling my handler behind me. He gestured for the others to follow.

Hunched over, the five ran to the soldier. As soon as they reached him, they kneeled, trying not to be seen. The orderly checked the wounded soldier's pulse and gently touched his forehead. The young man groaned in pain. I was glad to see he was alive.

"Head wound," the orderly whispered. Quickly he poured antiseptic on a wool pad and held it to the man's temple. Private Kent helped him tie a strip of bandage to hold the pad in place. The stretcher bearers carefully lifted the soldier onto the canvas sling. Staying low, they scurried off.

It was then that I heard a faint voice. "Hello? Over here!"

Private Kent had started after the orderly so I knew he hadn't heard the sound. I darted in front of him

and lay down at his feet. He frowned at me and jerked at the leash. "Darling, 'eel!" he ordered with another jerk. "We need to get back before we get killed!"

I refused to get up. I refused to obey. I knew there was another wounded man.

I gazed beseechingly up at my handler. His eyebrows rose as if he finally understood, and he unclipped the leash. I sped in the direction of the voice. I strained to hear it again, but now all was silent except for the drone of airplane engines overhead.

Confused, I stopped and glanced around the stark, shadowy landscape. Before me was a crater made by

an explosion. Around me was leveled ground. There was no sign of a person. Had it been the enemy trying to confuse me? Was I leading Private Kent into a trap?

"Hello? Down here!"

That was no German voice. Dropping to my belly, I peered over the edge of the crater. A soldier stared up at me. His leg was bent, just like Sergeant Hanson's had been.

I bounded down the gravelly side. When I reached the bottom, the soldier stroked my head. Tears filled his eyes. "You're a better sight than General Plumer himself," he whispered.

Private Kent half-slid, half-fell to the bottom. "Blimey, 'ow'd you get into this mess?"

"Germans shot me." The soldier nodded toward his arm. The sleeve was torn and soaked with blood. "Knocked me clean into this hole. The fall broke my leg, but tumbling down here saved me from getting riddled with bullets."

Private Kent opened my saddlebag and pulled out bandages. He cut off the man's bloody sleeve with his knife and cleaned and wrapped the wound.

"I'm Private Bingham, 3rd Battalion. Born and raised in Worcester."

"Private Kent."

The soldier gestured toward me. "And my guardian angel?"

"Darling, number 204, War Dog." I could hear the pride in my handler's voice. Frowning, he studied Private Bingham's leg. "I don't 'ave a splint. We'll 'ave to stabilize it with me bayonet."

I waited patiently as Private Kent worked on Private Bingham's leg. Occasionally the soldier bit back a cry of pain.

Closing up my saddlebag, Private Kent sat back. "Well, Private Bingham, you seem to be of 'earty stock. I believe you'll live." He looked at the soldier's leg, glanced toward the top of the crater, then cleared his throat. "If we can figure a way to get you out of 'ere," he added, "before the Germans send out a patrol and take the three of us prisoner."

"I'd rather die," Private Bingham said.

"That we agree on, chum." Private Kent helped the soldier to his feet. He clipped on my leash.

Private Bingham leaned heavily on my handler's side and hopped on one foot. With Private Kent pushing and me pulling, they made it halfway up the slope. But then they both slid back to the bottom. Private Bingham winced, trying not to cry out. Sweat beaded his forehead.

I nudged Private Kent's elbow with my nose. The sky was growing light, and time was running out. He peered at me for a moment, then took off his cap and gave it to me. Gently I took it between my teeth. Then he unsnapped the leash again and I clambered up the side. When I reached the top, I heard voices. Without thinking, I dropped in a hollow. A small troop was walking toward me. Their uniform trousers were gray, and when I heard a few murmured words, they didn't sound like the English soldiers.

*Germans.* And if they continued walking they would find the crater and Privates Kent and Bingham. I had to steer them away.

When they were almost on top of me, I streaked from the hollow, Private Kent's cap dangling from my mouth.

Urgent German commands filled the air. *Crack! crack!* My ear stung as if struck by a sharp rock. Twisting and turning, I raced toward camp, using ditches and rubble as cover. I was fast, but the enemy soldiers' aim was accurate and bullets singed my fur.

More shots zinged over my head—only these were coming from the direction of the British trench. "Let 'em feel steel!" cried a small troop of soldiers running into the clearing. I recognized some of the men from Company B. The Germans crouched, fired, and then retreated as quickly as they had arrived.

Sergeant Hanson was the first to find me. Taking the cap, he beckoned a small party to follow us.

When we reached the crater, the sun was rising. We were standing in no man's land, sitting ducks for the Germans. Everyone knew it, though no words were spoken.

Sergeant Hanson and three other soldiers slid into the crater while the rest stood guard. Private Bingham's eyes were shut and he was propped against Private Kent's shoulder. Sergeant Hanson and Private Kent made a sling with their arms under the wounded man's shoulders. Two other soldiers took his legs. It took them several tries to climb from the crater. But once out, they were able to trot to the Allied trench while the other soldiers guarded their rear.

A cheer rose up when we came into view. Two stretcher bearers climbed up the ladder and hurried over. Private Bingham was laid on a sheet of canvas and passed down into the trench.

Lifting me in his arms, Sergeant Hanson handed me to Private Kent, who had jumped into the trench. He collapsed against the dirt wall and I flopped on his lap. Tweed came up and we eagerly snuffled a greeting. Dust clung to her wiry fur, and I knew that she'd been busy that night, too.

I crawled from my handler's lap. My ribs ached where I had fallen and my mouth was dry. Someone brought me a tin of water and Private Kent a cup of tea.

"Two sugars in me tea and a crumpet, if you please," he said hoarsely. "And me dog would like beef Wellington." Rousing laughter rose up all around.

Sergeant Hanson inspected my ear. "You're now a wounded soldier," he told me. "I'm sure it's painful, but we'll patch you up."

"A Victoria Cross for Private Kent!" one of the soldiers called.

He shook his head. "It weren't me. It were me war dog, Darling. She's the one deserves a medal 'anging from 'er collar."

"Three cheers for Darling!" someone sang out.

Now that we were all safe, exhaustion crept through me. I closed my eyes and slept.

## CHAPTER 11

# "The Fight Is 'ere"

Early June 1917

The nick on my ear healed quickly. Zero hour—
the moment when the British would attack the
Germans on Messines Ridge—was nearing. The exact
time was kept secret, but soldiers and support staff
were ordered to begin preparations. Battlefield
rehearsal areas were marked, and the platoons practiced and drilled. Soldiers hauled out giant howitzers
and set them up under camouflage nets. Ammunition
was stocked, and bread was baked and stored. All the
activity reminded me of the bees on the cowslip
blooms on Portsdown Hill.

The Hill was still in my memory. As were the sheep, Rags, Robert, Katherine, and my cozy bed by the fireplace. But they were growing hazier each day. My time on the Front was spent in anxious waiting, then furious searching. There was little time to dream.

The British repeatedly shelled the German lines. Between shellings, they sent raiding parties to clear the enemy's trenches. Each night, I led Private Kent or Sergeant Hanson to the fallen. In three days, I found more than fifteen wounded soldiers. When they were tucked safely behind British lines, my job was done. Then I would eat heartily—and sleep.

One night we accompanied the 3rd Australian Division. The men were strong and their laughter was confident. The dog squad marched with the medical corps as we followed the Australians to the unit's jumping-off point. We then helped stock a Regimental Aid Post in an old bunker slightly at the rear. I was fetching a stick one of the orderlies threw when I heard the plop of a gas shell.

I let out a bark of alarm and Private Kent, who knew I would not break training, saw the canister. He began to holler and at the same time he yanked out our masks. I ran toward him, my eyes burning. This time I was glad to have the mask pulled over my muzzle.

"Tear gas!" one of the medical men yelled. More shells plummeted from the sky like giant hailstones.

Many masks were pulled on too late, and soldiers began to gasp. The command was given to advance from the area, and the Australians' march turned into

a gallop. Private Kent and I had orders to return to headquarters after the RAP was set up. Hurriedly we left. When the tear gas was far behind us, Private Kent took off my mask. I rubbed my muzzle and head in the dirt until they felt clean.

We got in late that night. Private Kent bathed my eyes, but they still stung and I slept fitfully.

When I awoke the next morning, I saw half-dressed handlers streaming from their tents. The men clustered around Sergeant Hanson. I stood at the entrance to my crate, at the ready. Soon we would be seeing action.

The handlers huddled for a long time. Finally, after Beast began to howl for his breakfast, the group headed toward the field kitchen. Private Kent brought me my food bowl. He wore no shirt, his suspenders black lines on his thin white chest.

"Darling, the fight we've been waiting for is 'ere," he said as he set down the bowl. I tucked into it, gulping the meat and bread.

"And a massive battle it'll be. Just think of it—if the battle were a bucket of water, then you and me, why we'd be just two drops," he explained. "The sergeant says there are over two thousand big guns and 'owitzers set up over sixteen kilometers. Enough to blow the Germans to Paris."

I licked up the last of my breakfast.

Squatting, Private Kent stroked my head. "The Royal Flying Corps will keep the Germans busy from the air with their Sopwith fighters, and the tanks will roll over them on land. You remember those Mark IVs, lass?"

I wagged my tail, wishing there had been more meat and less bread.

"There are seventy-seven of those clanking creatures. Only I'm betting the Germans have the same arsenal. I pity the poor soldiers who have to face 'owitzers, planes, and tanks with only a rifle..." His voice trailed off and he shook his head sadly. "We finally know that zero hour is 0300 tomorrow morn. I fear we'll be spending all the next day gathering what's left of those brave Tommies who think they can win against such weapons."

I had never heard Private Kent speak so long—and so solemnly. I laid my head on his knee and he ran his fingers through my fur. "You're the best partner a bloke could ask for," he said, speaking low as if he didn't want anyone else to hear. "I just wanted to tell you in case..." His voice broke. Quickly he stood, coughed behind his fist, and asked, "Ready for a brushing, girl? Sergeant Hanson wants the dog squad in tiptop shape."

I tossed my head playfully, trying to erase the sad look in his eyes.

"All right then," he said with a weak grin, "I'll get the brush."

When he left, I glanced at the crate next to me, where Beast was making a racket. His handler brought him breakfast and the hound leaped so high that he almost flipped over. The other dogs began leaping about, too. Tweed was the only one who didn't join in the excitement.

I left Beast to his meat and bread and went over to Tweed. We sniffed each other, and I could feel her nervousness. The searching had been hard on the Airedale. Her toenails were chipped and her eyes were dull. When she wasn't working, she paced in front of her crate, wearing a path in the earth. Even liver treats from Private Reeves didn't soothe her.

I whined low in my throat, trying to tell her that soon it would be over.

Or so I thought.

**CHAPTER 12**

# Find the Wounded

June 6, 1917

Once again the dog squad was assigned to the medical corps of the 3rd Battalion Worcestershire. The soldiers of the regiment greeted Tweed and me and the other dogs with hearty hellos, kisses, and pats while our handlers looked the other way. Orders were strict: we were not to be pets of the infantry. But this was a special time. Zero hour was only a few hours away. I could feel the tension in the soldiers' hugs. Not one of them knew if he would survive the massive assault.

The regiment assembled in trenches close to Nutmeg Avenue, where the soldiers had skirmished before. I thought of Private Bingham and the many other wounded soldiers I had found. Were they safe in hospitals? On a ship bound for home?

"Medical corps waits at the far ends of the front line," said Corporal Currell, the officer in charge. "Because these trenches are newly dug and there was no time for dugouts, you'll have to fashion your own shelter. You'll be safe there until needed."

Tweed and I were assigned the south end. With our handlers, we trudged down lines crowded with soldiers writing last words and fixing stew over little round stoves.

"The generals issued new Tommy cookers," one of the orderlies said with a roll of his eyes. "Hoping a bit of tea would make us forget they were sending us to the front line to die."

The stew smelled delicious and I licked my lips. Often Sergeant Hanson would bring me a tin, knowing it was my favorite. Finally we reached our post at the far end of the line. It was sparsely guarded by soldiers. A few nodded at us as our handlers found places to sit on ammunition cases under a ledge of rock.

"We're less than a mile from Messine," a young stretcher bearer said as he rolled bandages. He didn't sound like Private Kent. "Or what's left of it," he added bitterly. "The entire village has been bombed and burned to the ground."

"You're a Belgium lad?" Private Kent asked.

The young man nodded. "Messines was my home. We farmed here." He gestured beyond the trench. "It's hard to imagine these fields were once lush with sugar beets and barley. All our livestock? Gone. All the families? Bombed out. All the homes? Rubble." He shook his head sadly, then fell silent.

I lay down next to Tweed. Her head rested on her paws, but shivers racked her body. I slid closer, hoping to warm and reassure her.

Private Reeves checked his watch. "It's 0200 hours. One hour to go."

The tromp of boots signaled that more troops had arrived. Cookers and pencils were put away. Rifles and bayonets were readied. Private Kent checked that our gas masks were handy, then stroked my head.

The soldiers began to sing softly. Their voices rang up and down the trench, distracting us from what lay ahead.

*Bombed last night—bombed the night before.*
*Gonna get bombed tonight if we*
*Never get bombed anymore.*
*When we're bombed, we're*
*Scared as we can be.*
*Oh blast the bombin' planes from Germany.*
*Gassed last night—gassed the night before…*

Corporal Currell interrupted the singing and sent out a small scouting patrol. Silently, the six soldiers disappeared over the parapet. They hadn't been gone long before gunfire rang out in two volleys. I bolted to my feet.

"The lads must've been attacked," Private Kent whispered. "The Germans are close."

We watched and waited until finally five of the soldiers rushed back into the trench. "There was a small platoon of Huns holed up in a bunker. Private Jameson was hit," one told the corporal. "We couldn't find him in the dark. If he stays out there, the Germans will kill him or he'll be blasted to bits at zero hour."

Corporal Currell checked his watch. "We have half an hour to bring him back. Send a dog."

He looked at Tweed, but I leaped up in front of him, ears pricked.

Private Kent stood. "Darling will find 'im." He unhooked my leash. Holding me under his arm, he climbed the ladder and set me on the parapet. "Be quick, girl. Begone."

Nose to the ground, I tore off. Back and forth I trotted, all my senses at attention as I searched for the fallen soldier. The sky was still dark, but my eyes gradually adjusted. The constant barrage of gunfire from the British lines was deafening. I would have to rely on sight and smell.

How far could our soldiers have gone? The shots had seemed so close.

The barbed wire had been cut in anticipation of the coming assault, so I quickly passed through. The earth beyond seemed even more shattered. There was no sign of life. No green grass, no birds, and no wounded soldier.

I was taking too long.

Then my nose found a trail of blood. Swiftly I followed it to a shell hole. The soldier was alert. When he saw me, his eyes opened wide. He was holding both palms against the bloody spot on his thigh where he had been shot.

"Good dog!" he praised. I sat beside him as he rustled in my saddlebags for bandages and antiseptic. "If I can just wrap this leg to stop the bleeding, I can follow you back…"

I turned to go fetch the orderlies as I had been trained to do, but the soldier grabbed my collar. I could tell he didn't want me to leave. I didn't blame him. No one wanted to be alone in no man's land.

Looking at my tag, the soldier whispered, "Hello, 204. I'm Private Mike Jameson—"

His introduction was cut short by an unexpected silence. The *rat-a-tat-tat* of guns and *booms* of artillery had been constant the past few days. This sudden, deathly quiet was eerie.

Then I heard a faint sound: the trilling of nightingales as they sang before dawn.

My body quivered from nose to tail. Private Jameson held his breath. He hugged me to his chest as if for reassurance. "Heaven help us," he whispered.

**CHAPTER 13**

# Zero Hour

June 7, 1917

Seconds later, the whole world erupted. *Boom!* A huge explosion split the air. This was a new sound, one much larger than the howitzers we were used to. *Boom!* The second blast shook the ground beneath us, and the noise was so loud I cowered closer to Private Jameson. He bent over me as dirt and rocks hurtled into the sky and then fell to earth.

*Boom! A* third explosion ripped the sky and plumes of flame and smoke burst into the air.

Stunned by the thundering blasts, I shook all over.

"It's the mines exploding on the ridge under the

Germans," he whispered. "I heard rumors that our engineers have been digging tunnels for months."

An intense barrage of bullets followed the eruptions, as if ten thousand rifles were firing at once. *Zero hour.*

I scrambled from underneath the soldier. Dust and smoke swirled around our heads. He coughed and then stood shakily to peer from the hole. Though the sun had been rising, it seemed as dark as night. "Dog 204, I am as lost as a baby," he said in a low voice. "You're going to have to save me one more time."

Private Jameson crouched low and grabbed my collar. I led us toward the British trench. He winced with each step and I could tell he was in pain. But he did not stop to rest. We scurried across the scorched earth like frightened mice. Through the smoke, I could see ghostly images of soldiers rushing past us toward the German line. They stooped, fired, stood, and then disappeared into the gray haze.

No one paid any attention to a limping man and a dog.

Distress flares rose from the German line as the Allied artillery kept up a fierce hail of bullets. Then I heard shells rocket toward the British lines as if the Germans were finally fighting back. Several whistled close by, and the soldier and I flattened against the ground. Booms and bursts of dirt beyond us told me the enemy shells were hitting their targets.

Jumping up again, we continued across the barren

land. *Crack-crack!* The sharp retort of rifles came from behind us. *Crack!*

Suddenly, I felt an intense burning above my shoulder near my collar. My right front leg grew numb, and I stumbled. Private Jameson held me up. "Courage, 204."

Hobbling along together, we reached the barbed wire that protected the Allied trenches. All was silent beyond the wire barrier, as if every British and Australian soldier had raced forward to attack the enemy.

Ignoring the pain in my shoulder, I hurried through the gap in the wire. Private Jameson followed close behind. On the other side, I searched for signs of the trench. Had I gone in the wrong direction? I turned and my paws sunk deep into soft ground of a new crater. Startled, I jumped backward. I sniffed the air, smelling gunpowder, smoke, fresh dirt…and *the wounded.*

Yet there was no one in sight.

The gunfire had moved into the distance, and the nightingales began to sing again. A ray of sun peeked through the haze. The private had stopped beside me. "The trench should be right here," he whispered, as confused as I was.

Then I sensed what the last barrage of German shells had hit. Private Kent, Private Reeves, Tweed, Beast—had they all been buried? Furiously, I started digging.

Private Jameson gasped. Falling on all fours, he, too, began to scrabble at the dirt like a dog. When he unearthed a flat piece of metal, he used it like a shovel.

The dirt was laced with sharp rocks and shrapnel. My paws began to bleed. My shoulder ached as if it had been crushed by a wagon wheel. But I kept digging.

"I found something!" Private Jameson called. An elbow poked up from the earth.

We dug together. *Too slow. Too slow.* I had to run for help.

I raced in the direction the other dogs and handlers had gone just hours ago. I had to find someone, but thick smoked filled the air, and I couldn't see any sign of life.

"Darling!" Sergeant Hanson emerged from the haze. Behind him, a group of soldiers and orderlies hurried toward me as well. They carried shovels and entrenching tools as if they already knew about the cave-in.

I led them back to Private Jameson. He'd uncovered a soldier lying face down in the dirt, his arms sprawled as if he'd fallen from the sky.

It was Private Kent. I barked, not caring about orders, not caring about my pain. I heard a muffled return bark deep within the earth. *Tweed!*

"There are more!" Private Jameson called. With everyone digging, we quickly freed Private Kent. Sergeant Hanson turned him over. I licked the dirt from his cheeks, which were warm. Sergeant Hanson felt his pulse. "He's alive. Let's get him transported."

"Hello!" Sergeant Hanson called into a hole in the earth. Crouching, I peered into the dark. Private Reeves and two stretcher bearers looked up at us from a pocket of air protected by a section of the parapet that had not collapsed. Tweed was in her handler's arms. All four were coated in dirt, except for their eyes.

I wagged my tail. Private Reeves grinned. "Lord, you are a welcome sight!"

"We'll have you out in a shake, mates," Sergeant Hanson said. He backed up to give the other soldiers room. They dug carefully, not wanting to cause another cave-in. Private Jameson's face was ashen. The bandage on his leg was stained red. "Your war dog saved my life," he told Sergeant Hanson.

"She's our best." The sergeant frowned at the private. "You need medical attention. The orderly will escort you back to the RAP."

I went back to digging. The burning in my shoulder spread until my body was wracked with tremors, but I couldn't quit. Finally the hole was wide enough to pull the soldiers and Tweed out.

Tweed greeted me with a lick and nosed my shoulder. I knew she smelled my wound. I jerked away, desperate to uncover the others.

"It was Private Kent who saved us," Private Reeves

said as he was hoisted out. "He heard the shells coming. He positioned himself on top of us so we wouldn't be buried."

I limped over to check on Private Kent, but the stretcher bearers were trotting off with him toward a horse-drawn ambulance. As I started after them, Sergeant Hanson called me back. "No, Darling. There's nothing you can do now. They'll take care of him."

I hesitated.

"You are needed here to find the wounded," he continued, sounding tired. "Messines Ridge has been taken—but the battle is not yet over."

I looked at the ambulance, longing to go with Private Kent. The sergeant snapped a leash on my collar. "*Stay.* That's an order, Darling."

As much as I wanted to follow my handler, I could not disobey. I let out a whine, deep and sad.

Then I collapsed at Sergeant Hanson's feet.

**CHAPTER 14**

# A Strange Place

June 10, 1917

I woke in a strange place. I was in a wooden crate, but not the one I was used to. It was dark inside except for a reddish pink light coming through the slatted bars on the crate door. The air smelled like antiseptic and bandages.

*I* smelled like antiseptic and bandages. When I turned my head, I discovered white strips wound tightly around my neck and under my belly. My front paws were also wrapped in bandages. My fur was matted and caked, but there was no way I could clean myself. Moving hurt too much.

Where was I? Peering through the slats, I saw that I was in a barn. Stalls, each containing a horse, lined the long wall across from me. A thin-looking horse wore a patch over his eye. A brown and white cart horse had a bandage around his neck—like me. Another draft horse hopped when he moved in the straw. They whinnied hungrily, and my stomach growled as well.

This wasn't the barn by the kennels. It was too silent outside. I heard no barking dogs, shouting soldiers, or thundering guns. The barn doors were shut, but rays of sunlight slanted through the cracks between boards. I decided the sun was rising. If it had been setting, the horses would have been fed.

So it was morning, I was in a barn, and I *hurt.*

This must be where they took the wounded animals. The ones that had disappeared from the battlefield.

The barn door opened with a creak. The horses neighed excitedly and I lifted my head. A small man walked in, his shirt and trousers covered with a white bib apron. He was whistling a saucy tune. From my

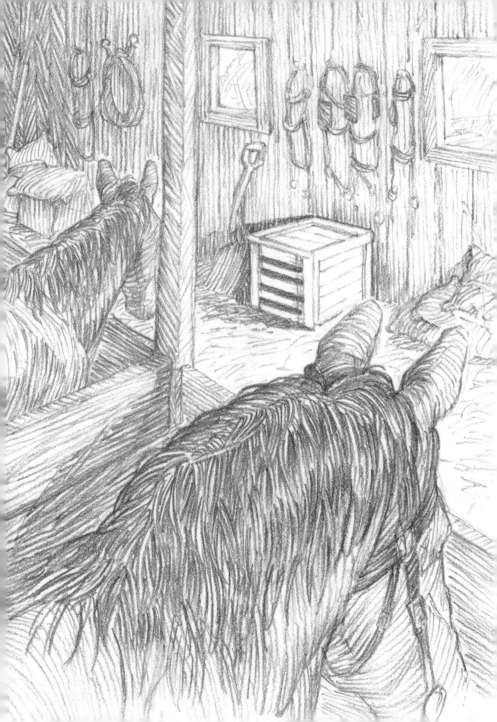

adventures with farmers and shopkeepers in Cosham, I had quickly learned that a whistling man was usually a pleasant one.

"Stop your bellyaching," the man said in a teasing manner to the horses. Picking up a pitchfork, he tossed each of them hay from a stack in the corner.

After he was finished, he walked over and peeked through the slats into my crate. His eye widened. "I see you've come to." Opening the door, he reached in. I shied from his touch. "Easy, now. I'm the one who's changed your bandages and tended your wounds, so don't fret. Private Jimmy at your service, 204."

He slipped a looped leash over my head and gently tugged me from the crate. I stepped out gingerly and stood for a moment, my legs as weak as if I'd just run miles.

"You've been several days without food or water." He set a pan of water under my nose. I turned my head away. Next he tried a tin of corned beef. I slunk back into the crate, lay down, and hid my head in the corner. Even though my stomach was empty, I didn't want to eat. And even though the man was being friendly, he was a stranger and I didn't want to please him.

Private Jimmy sighed. "I can't blame you. That's my own ration and I can barely stomach it. And you must have figured out I'm no dog person. Me, I was a jockey. That's why the army sent me to the veterinary corps." He chuckled. "Of course, I was used to being on top of a horse, not under one."

Private Jimmy gestured toward the stalls. "We're equipped for horses, not dogs. Though even there we fall short. Poor beasts. We humans know why we're in this bloody war, but those poor devils don't, do they? Yet so many of them get ripped apart by shot and worked to death."

I didn't respond.

Frowning, he shook his head at me. "The major had hounds. He'll know what to do with you when he comes." He walked away, leaving the crate door open.

I stared at the wooden wall, completely confused.

Where was Private Kent? Where were Tweed, Beast, and Sergeant Hanson? Had they disappeared like Private Jameson?

Pining for these men and dogs made me wonder about Robert and Katherine. Would I ever see any of the people who had once been important in my life again? Or would I disappear, too?

"This dog hasn't eaten since she arrived," someone said. It was the veterinarian they called Major. I knew him from his gruff voice, the white coat over his uniform, and his fondness for foxhounds. "Nor left the crate. It's as if she's too exhausted to eat."

"Her name's Darling." I lifted my head at the sound of my name. "And not only is she exhausted, she's probably in mourning." I knew that voice! The door was open and I peered out. Sergeant Hanson was staring in at me, grinning. "Hello, lass."

If I hadn't had bandages on my paws and neck, I would've leaped into his arms. Instead, I stood and wiggled in happiness from head to toe, causing every muscle to ache.

Kneeling, Sergeant Hanson wrapped his arms around me and hugged me gently. "I've missed you. The dog squad misses you."

I licked his cheek, telling him how much I missed them, too.

"Tweed and Beast and the other dogs, they're fine, as are their handlers," he said as he sat back on his heels. "The battle is mostly over, but they're still working."

I draped myself over his knees.

"Let me take a look at you, girl." He unwrapped the bandage around my neck and checked the wound. "You were shot just below the collar. We didn't see the bleeding under all your thick fur. Major Clemson gave you a trim and took out the bullet." Setting me on the barn floor, he stood up and asked sternly, "Now what's this about not eating? You can't get strong if you don't eat."

I tipped back my ears and hung my head. He pulled a tin from his haversack. "I brought you your favorite—beef stew." He spooned it into a bowl. "No excuses now."

It smelled as good as the bones we used to beg from the butcher. Hungrily, I wolfed it down and licked the bowl.

"What's her condition?" Sergeant Hanson asked the vet.

"The bullet that was lodged in her shoulder damaged muscle and bone," Major Clemson said. "We're trying to keep the wound from getting infected. Even if it heals, she won't be fit as a war dog again."

A sudden change came over the sergeant. His face paled and I knew that something was wrong. His hand dropped to my head. "Major," he finally said. "Can we keep that information between the two of us a while longer?"

Major Clemson nodded. "Of course. I've seen too many animals who served bravely labeled 'unfit.' The general says they can spare neither supplies nor time for animals that can no longer serve. I won't help the army add your dog to the list of those that will be destroyed. You have my word as an officer."

*Unfit. Destroyed.* I didn't know either of those words. But the sharp way the major said them made me hide behind Sergeant Hanson's legs.

That evening, I discovered what the words meant. Private Jimmy came in to feed us as usual. But this time, he didn't give hay to the draft horse in the last stall. Instead he haltered him and groomed him with care, muttering to him while he worked. The horse was lame—like me. I had noticed that he hobbled around his stall and often would only pick at his hay. Despite the attention lavished upon him, he didn't seem to be getting better.

Finally, Private Jimmy opened the stall door and led the horse to the doorway. Two men met him. Reluctantly, he handed the lead rope over to them. When they took the horse away, Private Jimmy hurried back into the barn. Then he began to sing at the top of his lungs.

Still, I heard the crack of a gun. The horse never returned.

**CHAPTER 15**

# Unfit for Duty

June 14, 1917

Sergeant Hanson traveled from the Front several times to visit me. The convalescent horse depot was far enough away that the sound of gunfire didn't reach us, but the road past it was often crowded with troops and traffic. No matter how noisy it was, though, I could always make out the roar of the motorcycle engine that announced the sergeant's arrival.

Each time he came he brought more stew. I tried to eat it to show my appreciation. Sometimes I had to force myself. Then he would clean my wound and put on fresh bandages before he returned to the dog squad.

On his fourth visit, he took off his uniform tunic the moment he arrived. After he had removed my bandages, he slipped a looped leash around my neck. "Time for a bath, Darling," he announced. "Major Clemson says your paws are healed. Your neck wound could use some soap and water." He wrinkled his nose. "Besides, you smell like bully meat left to rot."

He led me away from my crate for the first time since my arrival. I hobbled after him, my leg and shoulder still sore. For a moment I stood in the open barn doorway to enjoy the warm sun on the crusty gash on my neck and the cool breeze on my skin where my hair had been shorn.

A bath sounded good even to me.

Private Jimmy was filling a washtub with water with a hand pump. "I added hot water like you asked, Sergeant. Though it seems to me I haven't had a hot bath myself for weeks."

The sergeant laughed. "Nor I, Private. But I think we may get plenty wet right now."

I followed Sergeant Hanson to the tub. The muscles

in my shoulder were stiff, but something more was wrong with my right leg. It only moved a short distance with each step. I used to gallop up and down Portsdown Hill, but now I could barely walk.

Private Jimmy watched me with solemn eyes as I came closer. "It's a shame such a beauty has to be so thin and scarred."

"She's still a beauty," said the sergeant. Carefully, he lifted and set me into the water. At first it stung my still-healing wounds. But after a few moments it felt comforting.

The two men bent over the tub. I stood motionless as Private Jimmy ran warm water from a kettle over my back and Sergeant Hanson scrubbed me with a bar of soap.

Soon the water was brown. The final rinse was a cold shower from a hose. I shook, almost falling over when my wounded side gave way. Sergeant Hanson carried me to a sunny spot by a horse paddock. I rolled in the grass, waving my three good legs in the air.

After the sun had dried me, Sergeant Hanson led
me into the barn. He and Jimmy worked on my tan-
gles with horse brushes until I yelped for them to stop.

Then they stepped back and inspected me with serious expressions on their faces.

Neither man said a word. I wagged my tail, again wondering what was wrong. Suddenly a terrible thought struck me. The crippled horse had been given extra care, he'd been carefully brushed—and then he hadn't returned.

I sank down on the floor. I was lame. I wasn't going to get better. I knew my fate.

Sergeant Hanson put on his tunic. Slowly, he buttoned it. Then he slicked back his hair and set his cap carefully on his head. Private Jimmy brought my old collar, which he'd cleaned with saddle soap, and buckled it around my neck. The "204" stood out once again, no longer covered in dirt and blood. He gave Sergeant Hanson the leash.

"Godspeed," Private Jimmy whispered.

My heart began to thump as the sergeant led me from the barn. Balking in the doorway, I looked around for the two men who had taken the horse away. They stood by the side of the road under the shade of a tree.

But instead of handing my leash to them, Sergeant Hanson picked me up and carried me to his motorcycle. He set me in the sidecar. I whined anxiously and tried to scramble out.

"Sit," Sergeant Hanson ordered in a firm voice.

I obeyed, though I couldn't stop trembling. Private Jimmy waved goodbye as the motorcycle roared from the depot. We bumped down the road, weaving around marching troops and stalled tanks. Safe at the depot, I'd almost forgotten there was a war going on. Why should I care? Even though I wore my collar, I was no longer a war dog.

I had been deemed unfit for service. Only fit to be destroyed.

**CHAPTER 16**

# The Final Journey

June 14, 1917

The rough motorcycle ride jostled me and the ache in my leg grew worse. Sergeant Hanson wore goggles so I couldn't see his expression. But his jaw was rigid.

He turned off the road and stopped in front of a long, whitewashed building. There were several army vehicles parked outside, guarded by soldiers. A man stood by the front doors; he didn't wear a uniform. Sergeant Hanson parked and the man walked toward us, hand outstretched. A leather case hung from a strap around his shoulder.

"Good to see you again, Paul," the man said, shaking the sergeant's hand. "When was the last time? London 1914, after we beat you at rugby?"

"Good to see you too, Billy. And I believe it was our team that beat yours," he said. "So you know what we need to do?"

"Absolutely. And it will be my pleasure."

Sergeant Hanson began to lift me from the sidecar, but the man named Billy stopped him. "Let me get a shot first."

When I heard the word "shot," I flattened against the seat. But Billy didn't have a gun. Instead, he pulled a black box out of his leather case. Holding it to his eye, he fiddled with it for a long time.

Then I heard several clicks.

"Save your film," Sergeant Hanson said. "There will be plenty of great shots." This time when he picked me up, I could feel the excitement coursing through him. He set me on the ground and walked me into the building; I smelled blood and antiseptic. Confusion and fear mingled with my pain.

I balked again.

"It's all right, Darling," Sergeant Hanson assured me. "It will all be explained in good time. Heel."

Reluctantly, I limped beside him into a large, open room. Each wall was lined with beds packed close together, filled with wounded soldiers. A cluster of men in uniform surrounded one bed, hiding the man in it from view. Sergeant Hanson led me toward them, Billy right behind us.

A woman in a long dress hurried up. "Sir, dogs are not—"

Ignoring her, the sergeant walked faster. "Private Kent," he called out. "Private Kent!"

*Private Kent!* I knew that name. The group of soldiers turned in unison. It was then that I saw him. My handler!

Forgetting the pain in my leg, I bounded forward. Private Kent's face lit up when he saw me. "Darling! It's my girl!"

I tried to leap up, but my right front leg buckled under me. Sergeant Hanson caught me before I fell and set me onto Private Kent's bed. I licked away the tears of joy rolling down his cheeks. More cameras clicked and flashes of lights exploded around us.

Billy pushed his way through the crowd. "General! General!" he called out to a stately, white-haired man who stood in the middle of the other soldiers. "May I get a photo of you with the war heroes?"

The general glanced at the man, looking confused.

Billy pulled out a pad of paper. "Private Kent isn't the only hero who deserves to be decorated today, correct?" he said as he wrote something. "Darling, War Dog 204, was the one who found the buried soldiers."

"Aye, aye. It was me girl 'ere who saved me," Private Kent added. He started to say something else, but he fell into a fit of coughs, rasping and deep. I nuzzled his neck, willing him to stop. I had heard that cough too many times in the trenches.

Holding a handkerchief to his mouth, the general stepped away from us.

"She dug and dug...until 'er paws bled," Private Kent finally gasped when the coughing subsided. "She did it with a bullet in 'er side. We wouldn't 'ave been found if it wasn't for 'er and Private Jameson."

*Private Jameson.* I knew that name, too. A soldier on crutches hobbled over. I sat up and peered at him. Despite his clean face and smell, I knew it was the wounded soldier who had helped me dig out the others. Leaning down, he patted me. I licked his hand, overjoyed to find out what had happened to one of the soldiers I had only known for a short time.

"She saved me, too," Private Jameson said. "She took a German bullet for me."

*Click. Click. Pop. Pop.* Billy took photos of all of us.

Sergeant Hanson stepped beside him. "It's true," he said. "I was there. Private Jameson and Darling worked together to dig out the men from the medical corps. And Private Kent risked his life shielding them from the explosion."

"A photo of the heroes with you, General? For *The Daily Mirror.*" Billy waved his hand in the air. "I can see the headlines—*General Decorates Three War Heroes.* England needs uplifting news."

The general harrumphed but consented to stand next to the headboard. Private Kent sat up straighter in his bed. I raised my head proudly. When Billy lowered his camera, one of the soldiers handed the general two small boxes. He opened one and pulled out a shiny medal. "The British Royal Army thanks you for your service," he said quickly, as if trying to get it over with. He placed the medal and ribbon on Private Kent's chest. Then he did the same with Private Jameson.

Private Kent took the medal off his chest and tucked one end of the ribbon in my collar. "Please, sir, take a photo of the real hero to show all of England. Darling, War Dog 204."

*Click. Click. Pop. Pop.*

The general saluted, spun around, and left the room, his entourage in tow. A nurse came over to escort Private Jameson back to his cot. "The doctor tells me I'm on the mend," he said before he left. "Which means I'm heading back to the Front."

Sergeant Hanson raised one eyebrow.

"Which is fine with me," Jameson added. "I miss

my mates in the regiment." He gave me one last pat. "Take care, 204."

Billy and Sergeant Hanson watched him leave. "You can get the photos and story to *The Daily Mirror* this week?" the sergeant asked Billy.

"I'll take them to the correspondent's office myself," Billy said. "*The Wipers Times* has requested them as well. By tomorrow every soldier in the trenches will be weeping over this story."

"The general won't dare allow a hero to be destroyed." Sergeant Hanson burst out laughing as if he finally didn't have a care in the world.

"Will one of you explain what is going on?" Private Kent asked. Again he had a fit of coughing. I snuggled against his side, afraid to leave him.

Sergeant Hanson and Billy shook hands and the reporter rushed from the hospital. Then the sergeant pulled a stool over to Private Kent's bedside. "I found out that Darling was on the list of animals deemed unfit. She was to be destroyed today," he explained. "I had to figure out a way to save her."

Private Kent's eyes reddened and his fingers tightened in my fur. "I didn't know."

The sergeant reached for the medal still dangling from my collar. "Billy is an old chum who's a reporter for *The Daily Times*. He's making sure the world knows that both of you are war heroes. The army censors the news, but this story will get through. The British love their dogs and they've sacrificed them for the fight. The general knows that a photo of him decorating three war heroes is just what people need."

"A devious plan, Sergeant." Private Kent gave him a shaky grin. Then he clutched me tighter. "And now?" he asked. "What's going to 'appen now that neither of us is fit for duty?"

"Now we find a way to send Darling back to England." Sergeant Hanson ruffled my ears. "Your orders are to ship out in a week, Private Kent. Back to England to recover. I'm doing everything I can to make sure that Darling goes with you. I just need to convince my lieutenant that the British people need a returning war dog hero to celebrate."

Private Kent's grin widened. "Did you 'ear that, Darling? We're going 'ome." Leaning back against the headboard, he sighed happily.

I sighed too, and placed my paws on his chest.

"Do you remember the note on her collar when she arrived on the train at Shoeburyness?" Sergeant Hanson asked.

"It seems a lifetime ago."

Reaching in his pocket, Sergeant Hanson pulled out a stained and tattered piece of paper.

I nosed it, smelling a faint whiff of Cosham.

"*Dear soldier. This is Darling. She is smart and brave. Please take care of her and send her home to us. We love her even though she sometimes runs away. Yours truly, Robert and Katherine,*" he read. "Well, the children were right. Darling proved she was smart and brave. I didn't know then if I could keep that promise, but now I can."

Leaning forward, he cupped my face in his hands. "Darling, you and Private Kent are going home."

*Home.* I knew that word. Home had been a kennel, a ship, a train, a trench, and a crate.

But this *home* the sergeant was talking about was special. It meant that I would return to my beloved Robert, Katherine, and the village of Cosham. I wouldn't be able to run the hills of Portsdown ever again. But I would walk the village streets and greet the butcher and postmaster. I would watch over my family and keep them safe until Father returned. I would visit Private Kent and help him get back his strength.

And best of all, I would stay far away from this war. I had been the best war dog I could. But now it was time to go home.

Lifting my head, I barked and barked with joy.

# The History Behind
# *Darling*

## Dogs in the Military

Dogs have been used for war throughout history. During World War I, when *Darling* takes place, Great Britain and several other European countries used dogs on the battlefront. Soldiers discovered that dogs were loyal, smart, and quick and had keen eyesight and an excellent sense of smell.

The most common use for dogs during WWI was for carrying messages. A piece of paper was placed in a small metal container on the dog's collar. A dog could carry a message four to five times faster than a human across enemy territory. The fastest time recorded was three miles in three minutes! Dogs were also scouts, ammunition carriers, and guards. Ambulance and medical assistance dogs like Darling were used later in the war.

Training of these special dogs took about six weeks and required praise and treats like dried liver. First they were taught to heel, to sit, and to stay silent. All breeds were used, including mutts. Trainers looked for grayish or black dogs that would blend into the background on the battlefield.

## Mercy Dogs

Red Cross or Mercy Dogs like Darling searched for wounded men on the battlefield. They usually worked at night, using their sense of smell and superior vision. They ran through barbed wire, poisonous gases, smoke, fences, and explosions. "Good Red Cross dogs will quickly clear a battlefield of all the wounded soldiers," stated Senator George G. Vest (Scout, *Red Cross and Army Dogs*, page 17).

Mercy Dogs carried medical supplies and water to wounded men. If the soldier was unconscious, the dog would return to him, leading his handler and stretcher bearers. These dogs were trained to ignore dead soldiers.

Mercy Dogs were only used in World War I. When armies stopped trench warfare, the need for Mercy Dogs ended. However, dogs continue to be trained today in the military, often to search for explosives and drugs.

## Dog Heroes

Dogs proved their loyalty and bravery time after time in World War I. Captain, a French Red Cross Dog, found thirty wounded men in one day. Prusco, another French Red Cross Dog, found over a hundred men after one battle. Sometimes Prusco dragged soldiers into ditches, hoping that would keep them safe while he ran back to his handlers.

The United States did not use military dogs in World War I, but soldiers sometimes kept dogs as mascots. One of the most famous was Stubby, who became a hero after capturing a German spy. He was in seventeen battles and wounded many times. Stubby returned to America after the war. He was celebrated as a war hero and met three presidents.

Many brave dogs died in World War I. A 1917 issue of *Animals* magazine estimated that seven thousand war dogs were killed. There is a monument to dogs who served in the World War, 1914-1918 at the Hartsdale Canine Cemetery in New York. There is also a painting of Mercy Dogs by Alexander Pope in the American Red Cross Museum in Washington, D.C.

## Cool Dog Facts

✚ The Airedale was one of the first breeds to be trained for the military.
✚ A dog's sense of smell is fifty to one hundred times better than a human's.

✙ Gas masks for dogs were first developed during World War I.

✙ In 2011, there were over 2,300 military working dogs in the United States.

✙ A law was passed in 2000 allowing retired US military dogs to be adopted.

## A Soldier's Life

A military dog's life during World War I was tough, but so was a soldier's. At the Battle of Messines Ridge, most soldiers spent their days in trenches. They guarded the front line, which was the area closest to the German forces. In between was "no man's land," the ground that separated enemy from enemy.

Trenches were ditches dug in the ground, six feet deep by two feet wide. They were lined with sandbags, sticks, and metal. Support trenches connected to the front trenches in a twisty maze. Signs pointed the way, but soldiers joked about getting lost.

Troops shared the trenches with mice, fleas, frogs, and lice. "There are five families of rats in the roof of my dugout," British Captain Bill Murray wrote to his family, "which is two feet above my head in bed, and the little rats practice somersaults continuously through the night, for they have discovered that my face is a soft landing when they fall" (*The First World War: A New Illustrated History*, page 159).

When it rained, the ditches filled with mud. Soldiers on duty might have to stand knee-deep in water for hours. They often developed an infection called "trench foot." Another infection called "trench mouth" was caused by stress, smoking, and poor hygiene. "I have not washed for a week," wrote a soldier, "or had my boots off for a fortnight" (*Life in the Trenches*, page 69).

Food was carried from rear kitchens to the troops in the front line. Often it arrived cold and spoiled. Biscuits were so hard, reported a soldier, "that you had to put them on a firm surface and smash them with a stone" (*Life in the Trenches*, page 74). Soldiers were issued mess kits with fork, spoon, knife, and "iron rations" of tea and bully beef (canned corn beef) that they could heat over their Tommy cookers.

During the day, soldiers in the trenches played cards, wrote letters, and cleaned their weapons. At night, the Front became alive. Supplies were moved. Patrols crept from the trenches and scouted the area. Then raiding parties scurried across no man's land, crawling through barbed wire and darting into shell craters. Dodging machine-gun fire and bombs, they tried to capture and kill the enemy.

After one week to ten days of duty on the front lines, a soldier would be sent "to the rear." There they took a hot bath, washed clothes, and ate a good meal. "There is a bakery," reported a visitor, "where a Master Baker, in charge of a thousand men, bakes 350,000 2-lb. loaves every day" (*Life in the Trenches*, page 64).

## The Battle of Messines Ridge, 1917

As described in *Darling*, the Battle of Messines Ridge began with the explosion of nineteen underground mines. Rocks and dirt blasted high into the air. The earth shook and heaved. The explosions killed about ten thousand German soldiers. The noise and force even shocked the Allied soldiers (British, French, Australians), since the mines had been kept a secret.

Germany had controlled Messines Ridge, located in Belgium, since 1914. With the help of planes and tanks, the Allies were able to advance to the German front lines and capture the area. It was a bloody battle and a hard-fought victory for the Allies. It is estimated that over 42,000 lives were lost.

## Interesting Facts about the War

✠ World War I lasted from 1914 to 1918.

✠ It was named The Great War because it

was the first war to use massive weapons such as tanks and two-ton howitzers.

✠ "Bomb" is what the British call a hand grenade.

✠ A British soldier was called a "Tommy."

✠ Each soldier carried a ten-pound rifle, a bayonet, sixty pounds of ammunition, a digging tool, and a gas mask. Survival gear might also consist of eating utensils, bootlaces, a blanket, a razor, and iron rations.

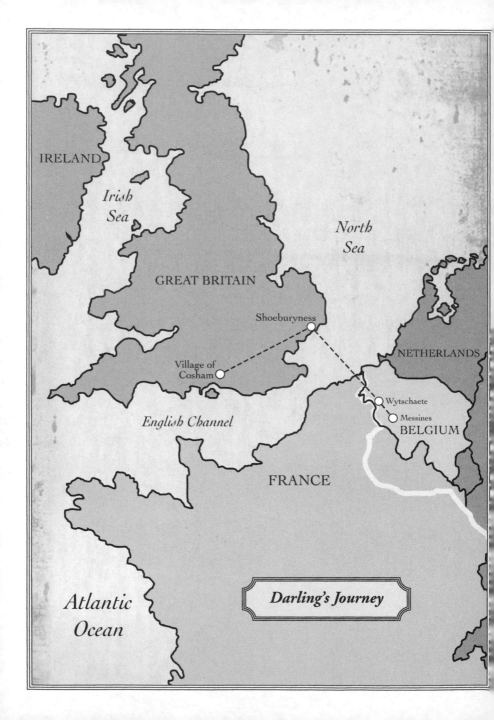

## Bibliography

Adams, Simon. *Eyewitness Books: World War I.* New York: Dorling Kindersley Limited, 2001.

Cooper, Jilly. *Animals in War: Valiant Horses, Courageous Dogs, and Other Unsung Animal Heroes.* Guilford, CT: Lyons Press, 2002.

Cummins, Bryan D. *Colonel Richardson's Airedales: The Making of the British War Dog School, 1900–1918.* Alberta, Canada: Brush Education, 2003.

Currie, Stephen. *Life in the Trenches.* San Diego: Lucent Books, 2002.

Freedman, Russell. *The War to End All Wars.* New York: Clarion Books, 2012.

Hamer, Blythe. *Dogs at War.* London: Carlton Books, 2001.

Jager, Theo F. *Scout, Red Cross and Army Dogs.* Rochester, New York: Arrow Printing Company, 1917.

Lemish, Michael G. *War Dogs: A History of Loyalty and Heroism.* Dulles, VA: Brassey's, 1996.

Passingham, Ian. *Pillars of Fire: The Battle of Messines Ridge, June 1917.* UK: Sutton Publishing, 1998.

Ross, Stewart. *Technology of World War I.* New York: Raintree Steck-Vaughn, 2003.

Ruffin, Frances E. *Dog Heroes: Military Dogs.* New York: Bearport Publishing, 2007.

Strachan, Hew. *The First World War: A New Illustrated History.* London: Simon & Schuster, 2003.

## FOR FURTHER READING

Adams, Simon. *Eyewitness Books: World War I.* New York: Dorling Kindersley Limited, 2001.

Freedman, Russell. *The War to End all Wars.* New York: Clarion Books, 2012.

Goldish, Meish and Ron Aiello. *War Dogs.* New York: Bearport Publishing Co., 2012.

Patent, Dorothy Hinshaw. *Dogs on Duty: Soldiers' Best Friends on the Battlefield and Beyond.* London: Walker Childrens, 2012.

Ross, Stewart. *Technology of World War I.* New York: Raintree Steck-Vaughn, 2003.

Ruffin, Frances E. *Dog Heroes: Military Dogs.* New York: Bearport Publishing, 2007.

## WEBSITES

Military Working Dog Foundation, Inc.
*www.militaryworkingdog.com/history*

A Multimedia History of World War I
*www.firstworldwar.com*

The Great War and the Shaping of the 20th Century
*www.pbs.org/greatwar*

The Worcestershire Regiment
*www.worcestershireregiment.com*

World War One Battlefields
*www.ww1battlefields.co.uk/flanders/messines.html*

Great War Photos
*www.greatwarphotos.com*

Royal Army Medical Corps in the Great War
*www.ramc-ww1.com*